TWISTS
"A corkscrew of a read"

Colin Youngman

Copyright 2017 © Colin Youngman

All rights reserved.

No part of this publication, paperback or e-book, may be reproduced, stored in a retrieval system, or transmitted, in any form or in any means – by written, electronic, mechanical, photocopying, recording or otherwise – without prior written permission of the author

ISBN: 9781520134550
ISBN-13:

DEDICATION

This one's for you.

Family, friend, or reader, none of this would be possible without your support.

Thank you.

CONTENTS

	Praise for the TWIST Series	i
1	Book One: DEAD Lines	1
2	Book Two: Vicious Circle	35
3	Book Three: Brittle Justice	56
4	Book Four: The Refugee	89
5	Book Five: A Fall Before Pride	121

PRAISE FOR THE TWIST SERIES

"A corkscrew of a read"

"Twists you won't see coming"

"Hooked from the very beginning"

"An incredibly talented author"

"Five stars - would recommend"

"Books you'll want to read again to spot the clues you missed first time round"

"Super dialogue"

"Fast-paced and thoroughly unpredictable"

"Great writing - I could visualise the scene".

BOOK ONE

DEAD LINES

CHAPTER ONE

Autumn. A time of year when the sun's low angle casts shimmering hues of gold and bronze over the rolling splendour of the Cheviot Hills, attracting the eye like a pendant to the charms of a full-breasted woman.

A ray of sunlight picked out the windshield of a silver BMW as it snaked its way around coiling country roads. A shard of light spun off it across the verdant valley, a searchlight sweeping over God's own country. The car hugged a tight right-hand bend causing a ram to scuttle a few paces from the unfenced roadside to safety. All else was still; the epitome of peace and tranquillity.

In the passenger seat of the BMW, things were anything but peaceful and tranquil. Jennifer North sat bolt upright. The tension in her shoulders and the grim set of her mouth betrayed the turmoil in her mind. Under different circumstances, she knew that this weekend would have been blissful perfection. Glorious weather, a Michelin-starred restaurant tucked inside a five-star country retreat, just her and her man away from the hustle and bustle of his stressful everyday life and her mundane housewifery. But Jennifer knew she had this weekend, and this weekend alone, to save her marriage.

And all the time, that…that 'thing' was lying on the rear seat.

The Northumbria Mansion House Hotel nestles in a cleft between two hills, cleverly positioned behind a small forest so as not to queer the view from vantage points across the valley. Its architectural design makes it almost impossible to see from the road, something the driver of the BMW realised as he suddenly came across its entrance.

The breeze from the open window caused Jennifer's mass of red curls to fan above her head like an Olympic flame as the driver executed a sudden left turn. The car fishtailed onto the long driveway, a manoeuvre that caused 'the thing' to bounce from the seat into the footwell, ever-closer to Jennifer. She cringed, recoiling from it as if something disgustingly repellent had wheedled its way between her thighs.

Jennifer ran her fingers through her tousled mane and decided she must confront the question that had been on her mind since she'd first laid eyes on the 'thing'. Unable to hold her tongue any longer, she steeled herself for the conversation she'd hoped never to have.

"Who's Paula, Stephen?" she asked.

"Hmmn?"

"I asked who Paula was".

"Don't know". Stephen applied the brake as they pulled into a vacant parking spot under the shadow of a towering, knotted oak tree.

"No? Are you sure?"

"Sure I'm sure. I don't know any Paula's". Stephen's gaze was fixed on a red squirrel foraging in the branches high overhead.

"Well", said Jennifer twisting to reach down and behind her, her seat belt snagging as she did so. "How do you account for this?"

Stephen's languid green eyes shifted from the treetops to the small, elegantly wrapped parcel studded with tiny silver-foil hearts, complete with pale blue bow, in the palm of his wife's hand.

"What's that?" he enquired with only mild interest.

"That's a good question. But it's not as good a question as mine. So, come on - answer it: who the bloody hell is Paula?"

Stephen rolled his eyes. "For God's sake woman – how many times do I have to tell you?"

"Oh, come on Stephen. You can do better than that. The label", she pointed towards a tag showing a couple of long-eared rabbits blissfully holding hands whilst gazing into a vermilion sunset, "says 'Happy Birthday Stephen'. It says 'All My Love, Paula'. It's got a load of fucking 'x's' on it. It's in your car, your name's Stephen, and it's your fucking birthday. It's happening again, isn't it? I'd accepted long ago that our marriage lines were dead lines as far as you were concerned but after everything you said when you finished with your last whore I'd almost started to believe we could turn this around. But you've gone and done it again, haven't you, you bastard?"

Jennifer flung open the car door. It smashed into the side panel of a Volvo parked alongside, leaving an obvious smear of silver paint inside an even more obvious dent. She attempted to jump from the car before realizing she hadn't released her belt. She cursed and slapped her hand on the red release catch. Her eyes blazed as she took her frustration out on the wheel-arch of the Volvo by stamping on it with her burgundy stiletto. For good measure, she repeated the act. Twice.

Stephen brushed the creases from his Armani suit as he followed her from the car, craning to see whether his own vehicle bore the marks of Jennifer's pique.

"For God's sake…what's got into you? Honestly, love; someone's winding you – winding US – up. Be logical. If that parcel was for me, and if it was from some…from someone else, don't you think I'd have opened it first? And don't you think I'd have hidden it somewhere, not leave it in full view? Why would I do that, on this weekend of all weekends?".

Jennifer was crying now. "To hurt me", she said softly. "To hurt me like you did last time. And the time before that. And probably countless times that I don't know about". Blood seeped from the corner of her mouth where she'd chewed on her lip.

"Aah, Jenny, darling…". He stretched a comforting arm around her shoulder.

Jennifer shrugged him off. "Don't you DARE touch me", she warned.

Exasperated now, Stephen snatched the parcel from her grasp. He tossed it into the air and, as it fell, volleyed it into the top corner of an imaginary goal net stretched between the trees. The squirrel hurried ever-deeper into the canopy.

"See?", Stephen pleaded. "It means nothing to me. I don't know what it is; don't care what it is. It's all a sick joke. It's got to be. I don't know any Paula's and I don't want any Paula's. I want nothing – nobody – but you, Jen. You've got to believe me".

But Jennifer was already striding towards the hotel entrance, head tossed back in defiance. Stephen hurried after her. The gravel drive crunched beneath their feet like crisp virgin snow on a frosty morning.

The sound of a twig breaking underfoot in the shadow of the trees went unheard.

CHAPTER TWO

The hotel lobby, all marbled floor, polished hardwood panels, and with an assortment of British wildlife adorning the walls, was a Cathedral of hushed reverence for the guests checking in. Even a party of Americans checking-out were subdued, for Americans.

The silence was shattered by the clatter of the revolving doors at the hotel's entrance as they spun like a carousel, such was the force of Jennifer's entry.

"Get away from me!", she said, twisting away from Stephen as he caught up with her and attempted to take her arm. "Just leave me alone".

"Jen. Please. Don't spoil things. This weekend's for us".

"Well you should've thought of that when you took that tart in the back of our car".

Heads turned in their direction. A spotty-faced concierge struggled to disguise his laugh as a cough.

"Keep your voice down!", he stage-whispered. "People are listening".

"It's not my voice you want to keep down. It's that thing in your pants that needs kept down".

A woman who looked too old to have mothered the child she was with covered her charge's ears in comic book fashion. "Do you mind? This isn't the time or place to air your soiled linen", she complained.

"Why don't you just piss off?", Jen retorted, much to Stephen's shame and the amusement of the woman's son.

"Well really", she spluttered, just as Stephen grasped Jennifer's arm more firmly this time and escorted her towards the desk where a receptionist was readying a 'Welcome' pack for them, desperately hoping to avoid the need for eye contact.

Jennifer stewed beside her husband while the receptionist talked them through the facilities on offer. Her mantra dragged on and, as Jennifer waited, she realized he might just be right. In part, at least. The delay had allowed her to think things through. She decided she didn't want a scene. What she did want, despite herself, was a husband.

As Stephen wrapped things up with the receptionist, he stole a glance at her name-tag. "Thank you, Svetlana. I'm sure we will enjoy our stay. You're a star".

The young Ukrainian beamed at him, both delighted and impressed that he knew the meaning of her name. The play on words was lost on Jennifer and when his attention returned to his wife, she managed to force a wan smile across her lips. She was determined to make this weekend work.

"That's better", Stephen said to her. "We'll clear this up later but I'm sure you know in your heart of hearts that all those things are behind me now. Yes, I've been a bad boy in the past. Yes, I've treated you badly in the past. And yes, thank God you've forgiven me in the past. But the past is exactly where all those things belong. I'm never going to give you an opportunity to NOT forgive me ever again'.

"Besides", he said, gauging Jennifer's mood, "the only Paulas I can think of are Abdul – I wouldn't be that lucky – and that marathon runner, Radcliffe. And I wouldn't be able to catch her!"

Jennifer slapped her husband in the chest, but it was a playful slap and her smile was genuine. It began to fade, though, when Stephen stopped and put a finger beneath his chin, a pensive look on his face.

"I do seem to remember there was another Paula, once, when I come to think of it", he mused. Jennifer closed her eyes and held her breath. "Yes, I remember now. Married a couple of rock stars. Was a bit of a celebrity in her day. What was her name, again? Yates. That's it. Paula Yates", he said. He afforded his wife an outrageous wink.

Jennifer let out the breath she'd been holding, but not before giving Stephen another playful – if harder - slap. "Geldof, actually", she corrected.

"Language", chided Stephen. This time her smile wasn't forced, and for the first time that day she actually laughed.

CHAPTER THREE

A sumptuous dinner, a bottle of merlot all to herself, an aperitif and a double Bacardi later, Jennifer was convinced they had been the victims of an ill-advised practical joke. Almost certainly one of his colleagues from the surgery, she decided. Stephen was forgiven.

Jennifer gazed through the picture window of the candle-lit lobby bar. It covered the entirety of the eastern wall. During the day, the view would be stunning. But now the sun had slipped below the horizon and, although it remained sufficiently close to cast an ochre glow over the moon rising bright and full in the evening sky, all that could be seen were the ghostly shadows of distant hills. She was tired, still a little emotional but, paradoxically, at peace with herself. 'Yes', she thought, 'the world's still a beautiful place'.

"I'm turning in", she said, extending her arm and squinting at her watch as she struggled to make out the pointers in the dim light.

"Already?", Stephen replied, automatically looking at his own Gucci SYNC. "Would you mind if I stayed for a nightcap? It's been a long drive and – err…shall we say 'a bit stressful' since!" He said it in such a way, with a smile on his face and in his voice, that his wife couldn't prevent herself from blushing with amusement, a little shame, and too much alcohol.

"Yeah, sure. It'll give me time to shower and get in the mood for LURV". She rose from her seat at the bar and kissed his forehead. "Sorry about before. I know I shouldn't be jealous but..."

"Hey, hey. It's OK. It really is. See you soon. I promise". He kissed her hand as she moved away.

Jennifer swayed slightly as she headed for the elevator. She glanced around self-consciously and was thankful that no-one had noticed.

She'd been the centre of too much attention already. She could just about cope with the other guests thinking of her as a madwoman, but a madwoman and a lush was on a different level altogether. The elevator door swished open at her touch on the button and she disappeared into its privacy with a sense of relief.

Alone with her thoughts, but at least still with her husband, she barely felt the movement of the lift as it transported her to the 4th floor. The ping of the bell announcing her arrival brought her to with a start. Flustered, she dropped her key card and, as she bent to retrieve it, mumbled an apology at a pair of scuffed brogues manoeuvring their way around her. She leant against the corridor wall to recover her balance and, in the process, knocked askew an expensive-looking oil painting. Her efforts to set it straight failed miserably.

"Bollocks", Jennifer muttered to herself. "No-one will notice"; the need to pee overwhelming her. Fortunately, she discovered that their room was next but one to the elevator and it was with some relief and no little surprise that she managed to swipe her key card at the very first attempt.

"Open sesame", she said as she melted into the warmth of the room.

Her urgency to pee dissipated upon seeing the enormous bouquet of red roses and pink carnations awaiting her within. The bouquet covered the expanse of the king-size four-poster that dominated the room. Their delicate perfume filled the air. Close by, set on a silver tray atop a Chippendale dressing table, sat her favourite bedfellows – Moet and Chandon – in a shimmering ice-bucket.

Her heart welled. How could she have doubted him? Sure, he could charm the birds from the trees, but as long as he didn't charm them into the back of his car, she could live with it.

She showered, imagined he was with her, and meticulously reapplied her make-up ensuring to add an extra red gloss to her full lips before stepping naked to the four-poster. She pulled back the satin sheets and smiled at the long-stemmed rose she found lying on the pillow. She held it seductively between her fingers, took in its fragrance, and clasped it to her. She winced as a thorn pierced her breast, causing a single drop of scarlet blood to fall onto the pillow.

She withdrew the bedsheets still further….and froze at what she saw.

CHAPTER FOUR

The air in the basement room reeked of body odour. There was neither natural ventilation nor lighting in its confined space. The only illumination came from the glow cast by the monitor bank affixed to the wall. Specks of dust circulated in the light they gave off, then drifted upwards like tiny bubbles in a fish tank.

Beneath the monitors, the console deck was cluttered with the usual tools of surveillance: discarded sandwich wrappers, empty can of Red Bull, half eaten pack of Oreos. There was barely room for his feet but they were there, too, legs crossed at the ankles. He watched the images with the intensity of a big cat stalking prey.

All six screens were switched on, as they should be, but the feed to monitor one had been inactive for several hours. Monitor two was labelled 'CP & E'. The image it showed alternated between the car park and a wide-angle view of the hotel's entrance. Not much to see here. The occasional flash of headlights as a vehicle exited the car park, but most residents had chosen to remain indoors tonight. The view of the entrance was even less inspiring; only a few guests or hotel staff emerging for a smoke every quarter of an hour or so.

Screen three showed an image from a camera installed within the lobby. It flicked between an internal view of the entrance and one of the reception area. He'd found this mildly interesting whilst Svetlana was on duty – he thought she was cute – but his interest had waned once she was relieved by a weedy specimen called Guy. Besides, shortly after this he had become fixated on screen number four.

His focus should have been on Screen Five; the one labelled 'BAR'. The feed for this monitor came from a camera situated in the lounge, always the busiest part of the hotel, especially once the guests finished dinner. Most incidents at night occurred here. But the exclusive nature of the Mansion House hotel and its clientele meant that there was little to note, more often than not, even here.

Screen Six was almost as boring as number two. Any other night, the image would alternate between shots of the hotel's corridors, fifteen-second bursts of each, and rarely showed anything more exciting than grainy images of guests leaving or returning to their rooms. He found it even less interesting tonight because the image was stuck on the fourth-floor corridor.

But it was screen number four that held his attention now, and had done for several minutes. Reflections of the image on the screen danced on his face like a silent movie. He held a polystyrene cup filled with lukewarm dishwater masquerading as tea halfway to his lips. It had been suspended there in limbo for almost a full minute. He stared at the screen, afraid to blink.

He was looking at a black and white picture but he knew the colour of her hair; hair that tumbled half-way towards the most curvaceous rear he'd ever seen outside of a photoshopped Kardashian. What grabbed his attention was the fact that the rear was naked. She'd been standing like that since she'd first stepped into camera shot. She seemed obsessed by something on the bed. He was obsessed by her.

"Turn 'round, girl. Just turn 'round. You can do it, you know you can", he whispered to the screen. And then, as if on cue, Jennifer turned and faced the camera. A little gasp escaped his lips. The semi he had harboured since she first appeared on screen sprung into something more substantial. "You beauty", he said.

And then Jennifer looked straight into the camera lens.

He sat up abruptly. Knocked some of the clutter off the desk as he retracted his legs. Dropped the tea into his lap. The camera was concealed – couldn't possibly have been seen – but it was if she was observing him, not he her.

He felt himself flush like a kid caught with his hand beneath the bedsheets. The heat burned his skin, irritated his face.

The concierge raised a hand and writhed at his pock-marked cheek.

CHAPTER FIVE

The candles in the Coldstream Lounge Bar had been extinguished, to be replaced by fingers of light from low-lux spotlights discretely sunk into the ornate ceiling. The overall effect remained low and subdued; a reflection of Stephen's mood. He perched on his barstool thoughtful and alone. He drained his glass and dragged the back of his hand across his mouth before ordering another beer.

As the barman pulled his pint, Stephen scanned the bar, taking in his fellow guests. The majority sat in booths, talking in tones normally reserved for a library. The bar was occupied mainly by couples, mostly older men with younger women. Stephen smiled at the irony of it. It seemed to him that he was the only one with nothing to hide.

Another lone guest approached the bar and took a stool three along from him. The man wore a suit but it was a cheap supermarket product and he stood out from the immaculately-suited or even tuxedo-wearing men elsewhere in the hotel. Stephen nodded an acknowledgement before pulling his i-phone from his jacket pocket, pretending to review his e-mails. He had no wish to become engaged in casual conversation.

After a while, Stephen slipped the phone back into his pocket. He knew he should go to his room where Jennifer would be waiting for him, but he didn't know which Jennifer he would be returning to. Her behaviour was developing into something increasingly eccentric. He took a long draw from his glass and decided to top it up with a final half-pint.

The bar had filled up as a steady file of residents returned from the restaurant. The lone barman struggled to cope, especially with several guests ordering coffee that had to be taken to their table. Stephen couldn't remember when barmen had first doubled-up as baristas but he found the trend for them to do so irritating beyond belief. A bar was to sit at, await service, then move aside. It wasn't a place to ask for cappo-mocha-latte-cino-frappe nonsense and expect it to be delivered where you sat. He quietly drummed his fingers, £10 note wedged between them, on the bar top whilst he waited his turn to be served.

The gleaming machine at the end of the bar gurgled and hissed as the coffee percolated. He casually checked his reflection in the mirrored backdrop and caught a glimpse of the lone man in the cheap suit. He seemed to be trying to catch his eye from between an optic of Blue Sapphire and a bottle of Jura single malt. Stephen looked away quickly, still not in the mood for idle chit-chat. He raised his gaze to inspect the ceiling; the one place where he wouldn't make eye contact with anyone.

"I bet you think they're random, don't you?" said a voice at his shoulder.

He closed his eyes and groaned inwardly. 'Here we go', he thought.

"What's that?", he felt compelled to reply.

"The spotlights". It was the man in the cheap suit. "You think they're random".

Stephen remained aloof to the stranger though he couldn't help but look at the spotlights in a more detailed way.

"Yeah. They're not in any pattern, now you come to mention it", he said, realising his mistake straight away when Cheap Suit leapfrogged onto the barstool next to him and continued the conversation.

"Aah, but that's where you'd be wrong, you see". A faint accent. Welsh, perhaps? "Look again. Tell me what you see".

Stephen looked overhead. "Well, there's one in each corner over there. A few others dotted around. Three in the centre of the room. A couple adjoined to those three, and we've got a string of them up here", he concluded, motioning towards them, "pointing towards the toilets at the back of the bar".

Cheap Suit's laugh carried the throaty hoarseness of a heavy smoker.

"Nope. Not quite as mundane as that, my friend. You see, we're in Northumberland, aren't we? Dark sky capital, so they reckon. Best place in the UK for stargazing, I'm told. And the lights in the ceiling; well, they depict the constellation Orion, the Huntsman."

Stephen knew who and what Orion was well enough, but he was sufficiently intrigued to let Cheap Suit continue. "I can't decide whether you're having me on here. Anyway, it sounds impressive. Carry on".

"The easiest way to tell it's Orion is those three lights in the middle. That's his belt, see? Now, look again at the lights pointing away from the belt….that's his sword. Notice how they're centred over the ceiling rose. That's not coincidental. The rose represents the Orion Nebular. And the ones right above us, they're his extended arm; they point towards…"

"…the toilets", Stephen interrupted, laughing. "Not very poetic, is it?"

Cheap Suit shook his head. "You still haven't spotted it, have you? On one night every month, they point…", he gestured towards the floor-to-ceiling window behind Stephen "…to that".

Stephen swung around on his barstool. The window could have been a giant cinema screen dominated by one thing: a vast full moon pressed against it as if a grotesquely bloated, acne-scarred face was attempting entry. And 'Orion's arm' pointed directly over his head to its epicentre.

Stephen's mouth gaped in awe.

"Wow." There was nothing more to be said.

Cheap Suit broke the spell. "Here comes the cavalry", he said, nodding towards a waif-like girl in crisp white blouse and black pencil skirt who had stepped behind the counter to help the overworked barman.

"Here; let me get them", Stephen insisted. "What're you having?".

"Cheers. I'll have an Irish. On the rocks".

Stephen ordered a Jameson's and a bottle of Corona for himself. The girl didn't look strong enough to pull his preferred cask ale.

"Stephen North", said Stephen, offering his hand. The stranger took it and told him his name was Stonebank.

"You here for the conference, too?", Stonebank enquired. Stephen tried not to show irritation as Stonebank crossed his legs and a muddy brogue brushed the trouser leg of his suit.

"Me? No, no. Birthday treat. From the wife. She's upstairs. I say 'treat' - I'm not altogether sure I didn't mishear her. She might have said 'birthday threat'. We're sort of getting to know each other again, if you get my drift, but it hasn't exactly got off to a cracking start".

"Aah", Stonebank nodded knowingly. "I see what you mean. Thought you looked a little down in the mouth, I did".

Stephen smirked humourlessly.

"Did I say something funny?"

"No. You definitely didn't say anything funny, believe me. I've heard it a hundred times. 'Down in the mouth': I'm a dental surgeon. Oldest joke in the book".

Stonebank smiled. 'Plenty work for me there', thought Stephen, casting an experienced eye over Stonebank's yellowing gravestone teeth.

"I'm only saying' it looks like you're doing well out of it, though", Stonebank commented with a nod to the Armani.

"Oh yes. Stressful 'til I got myself established but once you manage to set up in practice and find a niche, you've pretty much got it made. Got to be a bit routine now, if I'm honest, but falling into it was the best move I ever made".

"So it's not what you've always done, then?"

"It is, but by default. I've sort of got Jennifer – my wife – to thank for it I suppose".

"Really? How come?"

Stephen regretted starting this conversation now but it was too late to back out. He took a deep breath and continued.

"Well, I was lucky that my parents gave me a really good education. I studied hard, very hard, but everything else fell into place. Without sounding boastful, I could probably have taken any course at any uni I chose. But I was sick of studying. I wanted something that I thought I could enjoy. So, of all things, I enrolled on a Drama and Media course. Naturally, my parents were appalled…"

"Hang on, time out, time out". Stonebank made a T with his hands "Let's rewind a bit. You're telling me that you stick a pair of rusty pliers into people's mouths on the back of a degree in Luvvey-ness?"

"Oh no. The drama thing lasted less than a year. That's where Jennifer comes in. I met her on the third night of fresher's. I was in a club when I first saw her. She had her back to me and she was wearing this incredible red dress that showed off her curves. But that's not what first drew my attention. Jen's always had this fabulous thick tangle of red hair, and this particular night she had it all piled on top of her head". He smiled at the memory. "Unfortunately for her", he went on, "she was standing right under an ultra violet light. It drained all the natural colour from her hair and replaced it with a kind of bluish-purple. So I went up to her and told her she looked just like Marge Simpson".

Stonebank laughed. A globule of amber whiskey escaped his mouth and dribbled down his chin. He flicked his tongue in a failed attempt to retrieve it. "Not the best chat-up line I've ever heard, my friend".

"Too true. Anyway, it turned out she was on the same course as me. A few months on, we started dating. By this time, I'd already discovered from our work in class that she was a brilliant actress. A real natural. Probably would have made a career of it if we hadn't married so early".

He halted for a moment, caught up in his memories. "Where was I? Oh yes, she was far better than I'd ever be and, after always being the best at everything I'd done up to that point in my life, I couldn't stand the thought of coming second. So I had a word with the dean and managed to change courses. The rest, as they say, is history".

Stonebank nodded. "But why dentistry? What drew you to that?".

"Simple, really. The lecturer was smokin' hot!"

The man in the cheap suit slapped Stephen on the back and laughed until he coughed.

"So, what about you? What business are you in?", asked Stephen, wanting to talk about someone else's shop rather than his own, especially on his birthday.

"Self-employed, I am", Stonebank answered. "But as far as the taxman and the job centre's concerned, I'm unemployed. I guess", he said, looking at the moon, "there's a part of Orion in me. Bit of a hunter, see? Whatever contract I'm on, the gaffer tells me what he wants and I hunt it down for him".

Stephen nodded. A gopher, he thought. He knew anything he said would sound patronising so he said nothing at all. He had no reason to offend his companion.

"'Nother drink?" asked Stonebank, sensing Stephen's unease. "Or are you on a curfew?"

Stephen checked his watch. "Why not? We're not quite at the stage where she gives me deadlines. Not yet, anyway. Besides, she'll only want me more the longer I keep her waiting!" They both laughed, and the barman set up two more drinks on the counter.

CHAPTER SIX

Stephen giggled like a schoolboy. He didn't know why he found the sight of a skew-whiff painting outside his room funny, but he did. He assumed it had something to do with trading drinks whisky-for-whiskey with Stonebank for the best part of an hour.

The Home International of drinking bouts, Englishman on Scotch, Welshman Irish, ended in an honourable draw. Stonebank tried to claim victory, stating that as the hotel was in England he should win on the rarely-cited away drinks rule, but Stephen would have none of it.

He had left Stonebank in a mock sulk to return to Jennifer. He hoped she wasn't in the arms of Morpheus. He found the key card in the third pocket he tried, swiped it upside down the first time and then with the chip facing outward before finally getting it right. The door opened an inch or two.

"Aah'sa comin', honey-child', he crooned through the widening crack. "And aah'sa got summat for ya".

Stephen slipped through the door and flicked on the light-switch just as a champagne bottle exploded on the wall above his head.

"What the…."

"You bastard", shrieked Jennifer. "You utter, utter, BASTARD!!".

Stephen caught a glimpse of her, dishevelled hair, black streaks of mascara running down her cheeks, over-red lipstick smeared across her face, as she lunged at him, fists flaying.

His first thought was that she'd auditioned for a screening of a death-metal rock video. Or Zombie Apocalypse. One of the two. He didn't have long to decide which for she was on him in an instant. He felt long nails gouge his cheeks, a flume of spittle stung his eyes, temporarily blinding him. He closed his eyes; a blessing because a second later the blindness would have been permanent as her fingers reached his eye sockets.

Stephen sobered instantly. "Hey, hey – stop it. STOP IT!". He tried to pin her arms to her side. She jerked her head forward and went for his face with her teeth. He released her arms and held her head in his hands. She started punching again. Stephen managed to grab both her wrists in one hand. He pushed his other forearm into her throat to keep her head at bay.

"For fuck's sake, Jen…." was all he managed to say before the wind was taken out of him by a knee to the groin. He reacted reflexively, his fist ramming into the solar plexus of the banshee that was his wife.

She staggered back onto the bed where she lay sobbing, panting, cursing and all combinations in-between.

The occupants of the room next door banged on the wall. "Sorry", Stephen said to the wall, hoping he spoke loud enough for their neighbours to hear.

"No he's not! He's never fucking sorry. For anything", Jennifer shouted, leaving no room to doubt that they heard her.

"Jen. For Heaven's sake. What's up with you? Have you been drinking or something?" He wiped a stream of blood from his cheek.

"Drinking? Would you blame me if I had? Bastard. You've been with HER, haven't you"? Jenny pointed to something on the pillow alongside her. Stephen followed the path of her finger until his gaze came to rest on the sight of a familiar, if now damaged, package.

"How'd that get in here?" he gasped, incredulously. A further message had been added by the same hand. 'See you tonight. Don't be late. P. xxxxx'. He felt the hair on the back of his neck stiffen and his flesh crawl.

"Get out of my sight", Jennifer hissed.

"But darl…"

Stephen cut the word short as the ice-bucket followed the route of the champagne bottle.

"Get out. Cheating louse. Get out! GET OUT!!"

Stephen beat a hasty retreat as Jennifer reached for the tray. Outside, the corridor was filling with guests pouring from their rooms, some pulling on robes.

"I'm sorry about this. She's not been well", Stephen lied by way of explanation to the duty manager who had arrived on the scene, although Stephen feared it may not be a lie at all. "She'll be ok in a moment, I promise. Darling, are you alright?" he asked from outside the closed door.

"Bastard!"

The onlookers shook their heads in disgust. "Sorry", he said to them. "I really am".

He knew he'd not get back in the room. Not tonight. Not with Jen in this state. The crowd dispersed as he tucked his shirt back in and caught the lift down to the bar. Several guests returned to their room. Most followed him to the bar as if unwilling to miss the next instalment.

"Better than EastEnders", said one microskirted blonde to her grey-haired companion.

CHAPTER SEVEN

Stephen sat hunched over his replenished pint as he recounted the evening's events to Stonebank, who had returned from a cigarette break outside. Stephen didn't think he'd ever been so relieved to see anyone. He had felt totally exposed and vulnerable sitting alone, all eyes on him. Like in one of his childhood dreams where he was dressed in nothing but a T-shirt that didn't quite cover his modesty.

"So how'd it get back into your room?", Stonebank asked.

"God alone knows. But someone doesn't like me, that's for sure". He picked a paper drip mat from the bar top and held it against his clawed cheek.

"Must have one hell of a grudge against you to go to all that bother", Stonebank surmised. "Why not just smash your windscreen, key the paintwork, slash your tyres – something like that? Hell, they could have done all three and it would be easier than breaking and entering".

Stephen stared into his glass. He shrugged. "Beats me. I could cope with the car if they'd done that. But to bring Jennifer into it – why do a thing like that?".

"I'm telling you there's some crazy people in the world, my friend", Stonebank added. "And it doesn't pay to cross them".

"But I haven't crossed anyone. I can't for the life of me think why anyone would do this. I don't owe money, I haven't tread on anyone's toes in business, no-one's filed a lawsuit against me for botched dentures. None of it makes any sense".

Stonebank thought for a moment. "Of course, you could be coming at this from the wrong angle".

"Go on…"

"Maybe it's not that someone doesn't like you. What if someone likes you very much? Say, way too much?".

Stephen frowned at him. "Waddya' mean?".

"Well, it seems to me that this Paula woman has a real thing about you. To go to all this trouble…"

"You haven't listened to a word, have you? I wasn't lying to Jenny. There is no 'Paula woman' – she doesn't exist".

"No? Come on, you can tell me. We're both men of the world, see. We know what it's all about, don't we?"

"What is this? You're as bad as Jen".

Stonebank pulled his bar-stool nearer to Stephen. It screeched on the parquet flooring. Heads turned in their direction. Stonebank lent in, his face so close to Stephen that his rancid whiskey-breath washed over him.

Stephen recoiled. "Get away from me!". His voice was an octave too high. More people were watching now, their conversations hushed. Stephen felt his face begin to flush.

Stonebank's yellowing teeth were barely an inch from Stephen's face. "Oh, I'll get away from you, alright. I'll get away from you when you get away from Paula. Where've you got her hidden? Booked another room for her, have we? A nice little love-nest, I bet. I think we're overdue the truth from you, aren't we? Well overdue".

Where once Stonebank had represented a faintly pathetic figure, he was now the personification of menace. He stared unerringly into Stephen's eyes. Nicotine-stained fingers reached up to stroke the lapels of Stephen's suit. They sat silhouetted against the moon, actors on a stage picked out by limelight. People moved closer like an audience filing into an auditorium.

"You're a bloody lunatic!", Stephen said. "This has nothing to do with you anyway".

"I beg your pardon but this has EVERYTHING to do with me. I told you before, didn't I? When my boss wants something, I always – that's ALWAYS – get it. And right now, my boss wants Paula back. Back where she belongs".

Stephen shook his head. "I don't believe this is happening. And it's not funny anymore".

He laid a hand on Stonebank's shoulder as he levered himself off his stool. Stonebank slowly looked at the hand, then just as slowly returned his gaze to Stephen's face.

"This never was funny, my friend. And I suggest you never touch me again".

There was a flash of steel as moonlight caught on the blade that Stonebank produced from somewhere within the crumpled suit. It was at Stephen's throat before he could move.

"Stephen North", Stonebank leered, "Meet Orion".

The 'audience' gasped. One woman's scream was stifled by her partner's hand over her mouth.

"See", he continued. No-one's going to help you. They're all too scared".

Stephen looked around the sea of grim faces; faces awaiting a public execution. The concierge who oversaw Stephen and Jennifer as they checked in was there. It seemed to Stephen that he was still trying to disguise a laugh.

He recognised guests who had been in the corridor when Jennifer threw him out. They looked on but none came to his rescue. The duty manager had made his way downstairs, too, but didn't intervene.

He saw the aged mother who Jennifer had affronted. She watched quietly. The person next to her had his mobile phone out recording the scene. Recording, for heaven's sake, but doing nothing to help. Stonebank was right. No-one would come to his aid.

"So, my friend. For the very last time, where's Paula?"

Stephen swallowed hard. He felt the blade bite into his Adam's apple. Perspiration glistened on his forehead. "I swear. I don't know. You've got to believe me. I don't know".

Stephen was drowning in the stench of his own fear. Wide-eyed, he swung one last look around the room in search of a saviour. And there, framed in the doorway, he found her. Jennifer. Freshly made up. Dressed in red. An outfit that seemed vaguely familiar. Her hair was stacked high on her head.

"Oh God. Thank the Lord, thank God. Jennifer, darling, tell him. Tell him I'm not lying". He almost laughed with relief.

A strand of Jennifer's hair came loose. It came loose because she had shaken her head.

"That, my friend, was your last chance", Stonebank.snarled.

Stephen was paralysed by distress. He felt a warm trickle of urine run down his leg. He tried to speak but no words came. It didn't matter. He couldn't have spoken anyway. The knife had already severed his vocal chords as it sliced its path across his throat.

For a moment, Stephen could have sworn he heard a ripple of applause. Then he realised it was the thick, wet splats of his arterial flow as it pumped against the window. The moon turned a sickening red.

CHAPTER EIGHT

Jennifer closed the door behind her. She leant back against it, head to one side as if listening for something. Her heart pounded, pulse raced. Her breathing came in short sharp gasps. She grew light-headed. Jennifer recognised the signs. Hyperventilation. She recalled a technique she had been taught in therapy many years ago. She forced herself to take in a long deep breath. Hold it for three seconds, she remembered, then breathe out slowly, counting to three. She repeated the act, then once more.

It was on the third exhalation that she heard it. Footsteps, indistinct at first, moving along the corridor towards their – towards her – room. A cough outside the door. A couple more footsteps followed by a barely-discernible scratching noise; the sound of a painting being straightened on a wall. Then the footsteps moved away more quickly, the lift call pinged, and there was a faint mechanical whir as the elevator began its journey down the shaft.

Jennifer finished the exhalation, smiled, and moved away from the door. She reached into her clutch back, shunted a few tissues to one side, searched beneath her passport and the ubiquitous sanitary ware, and withdrew her mobile phone before taking Radley for a walk back along the zipper.

She flung herself on the bed. She was buzzing. Her ears sang with the adrenalin rush but at least she was back in control of her breathing. It was gone two a.m. but she had to talk. Jennifer flipped open the cover of her mobile and speed-dialled the number.

She rocked back-and-forth on the bed, unable to settle, whilst the phone rang out. Just when she was sure the call wasn't going to be answered, it was. She heard a sleepy voice on the end of the line.

"Hi sis. It's me. God, what a night. You wouldn't believe, you really wouldn't, sis", she gabbled.

It slowly dawned on the disembodied voice on the other end of the line who was calling. After a lengthy yawn, the voice asked if things had gone smoothly.

"Couldn't have gone better. Went exactly as planned. I'm soooo excited. I really think that, this time, I'm onto something big".

Her sister asked how she'd set it up.

"Well, it took a helluva lot of planning but everything paid off. I had to do all the arrangements myself, as you know. I e-mailed everyone involved, researched the equipment I'd need, found the right location – all that sort of stuff. But it all came together beautifully on the night". She was off the bed again, prowling her room.

"Come on, then", her sister asked now she was wide-awake. "Tell me all about it, Jennifer".

"It started before we'd set off. I miked up the car and set a micro-camera up to catch the action. We had cameras and mics in the lobby, bar, the corridor, our room; everywhere, really, in the hotel. The hotel staff couldn't have been more helpful. They always had someone in the transmission room for us. We explained when we wanted them to switch camera shots and they arranged for the action to be transmitted to the bar and guest's rooms. Their staff and the guests who had parts were told what would be happening when. We set them up with their own little microphones; all that stuff. Am I making any sense, sis? I'm not really thinking what I'm saying here. I couldn't be higher if I'd snorted a line!"

Her sister laughed and told her that she wasn't really making much sense but to carry on anyway – she'd catch up, she was sure.

"The guests really bought into the interactivity of it all. The feedback from them was brilliant. They really felt part of the action. Said it took Murder Mystery weekends to a new level. Which, of course, is EXACTLY the reaction I was after. Anyway, I'm on a real winner here. Got lots of plans to take this worldwide. I'm on a flight tomorrow, actually".

"I'm so pleased for you, Jen. You really deserve this. So there's just the three of you involved, then, is there: you, Stephen and what's-his-name?"

Jennifer was back on the bed, twisting her hair into ringlets between her fingers.

"Yes. And I'd forgotten how good Stephen was. I mean, SERIOUSLY good. He always played down his acting skills at uni but he shone tonight, he really did".

Her sister said she was surprised, and asked whether Stephen would be prepared to gamble his career on her business plan.

"Do you know; I really think he would. I know him well enough by now to safely say he had a whale of a time. And I know he's been looking for something else to stimulate him. The routine of his practice was getting a bit too… well - 'routine'. You know how easily he gets bored; always looking for some new interest. He wouldn't be bored with this, I tell you. The buzz is incredible". Jennifer bounced off the bed and paced to the window. She looked out. There was nothing to see so she flopped back on the bed.

"I think you're taking a big risk, Jen. I mean, it worked this time, but surely you're so reliant on the guests not mucking up their lines. You three are professionals or at least have had professional training, but the others…"

"No, no, it's not scripted as such. That makes it even more exciting It's improvisation. I prepared a storyline for us – a detailed one, I admit – but then we just went with the flow".

"But the guests…"

"Yeah, they have lines of dialogue but pretty basic ones. You couldn't call it a script. Mostly it's just directions. We'll say to them, when this happens, do that; go there; that sort of thing. And if they do have to speak, we let them know in advance when they need to come in".

"So how does that work?"

"Well, we don't tell them the full storyline because we want them to be carried along by it. But we let them know when they need to 'act'. We ask them to listen out for a sentence and when they hear it, they know it's their turn to speak. We call them our dead lines because after we've spoken them, our action stops".

Jennifer rummaged in her bag, still unable to keep still. She pulled out her lipgloss, removed her passport, applied her lippy. Put it away again.

"I still think it's something to you need to be careful about", her sister cautioned. "It must cost a pretty penny to set it all up, with no guarantees at the end of it".

"I know. But I need something more in my life. Sitting at home all day..well, I'm going stale. I need to exercise my wings. You're right about the cost but we've got Stephen's money to fall back on. And besides, most of the costs are one-off upfront expenses for the hardware and software costs for the cameras and such like. The only ongoing costs will be for promotion and marketing. There'll be some surprises for us along the way, I'm sure. For example, one of the biggest spends this time went on special effects. You should have seen them, though. I tell you it was worth every penny. Seriously, the blood and gore was truly spectacular."

"I'd rather not see it, thank you very much. You know I can't even watch Casualty on TV", her sister laughed. "Anyway, is Stephen around? I'd like to hear his Oscar acceptance speech".

Jennifer was at the window again, looking out. A car sat with its engine idling. A figure stood alongside it beneath a streetlight. Smoke curled towards the light, the glow of a cigarette end barely discernible.

"'Fraid not, sis. You know what these ac-tors are like", she said, drawing out the last syllable. "He's still down the bar. Or the Green Room, as I bet he's calling it now. He'll be referring to everyone as 'dah-ling' already". They both laughed. "I should probably head down to the lounge myself, actually. 'My public awaits, you know'. Besides, if we're flying out tomorrow, I need to rescue him. Can't afford to miss the flight and he must be off his face by now. He's been celebrating his success in the bar ever since his performance ended". She walked out of the room towards the lift.

"That'll be good, Jenn, cos If you stay on the line, I'll chat to Stephen when you get down there. If he's coherent, of course".

"Yeah, that'll be fine. Hold on, then". She pressed the button marked '0' on the panel inside the elevator. The doors swished shut. "So, anyway. How's Doug? Guess he's a bit grouchy at me for waking him up".

She pretended to listen to her sister whilst the lift shuddered downwards. The Chillingham Restaurant was to her left as she exited the elevator, the bar on her right. She took neither. Instead, she stepped past a deserted reception and headed straight on towards the revolving doors.

"Nearly there, sis. Just need to find him in this crowd". She was outside. The night-time chill caused her to shiver. "I'm going to pretend I'm angry with him when I see him. He hasn't even called me since the show ended, never mind see me. I don't mind really – he's been so wrapped-up in his performance – but he doesn't need to know that. It'll be a laugh".

She opened the car door. Almost before she'd hit the seat, it was in gear and pulling off. She wrestled with the seat belt one-handed.

"I can't see him anywhere at the moment, sis. It's as if he's disappeared into thin air. Unless he really has been 'murdered', of course. That'd explain it. Wouldn't it, Paula?".

The line went dead.

*****

Look out for:

DEAD Heat

The full-length novel sequel to DEAD Lines

BOOK TWO

VICIOUS CIRCLE

ADAM

He always exercised early. He didn't see why today should be any different yet, as he took his first powerful strides, the beads of perspiration that dampened the bandana around his brow were those of a cold sweat. Today WAS different.

He sprinted across the cobbled courtyard and squinted up at the bell-tower, at its rampant lion, and at the legend 'Ad Augusta per Angusta' unfurled beneath it. 'To High Places by Narrow Roads'. How apt. Possibly. He looked at the clock-face. Seven-ten. By the time he returned, he would know.

He adjusted his stride pattern and settled into a steady rhythm. Ironic that he felt most at home on the roads when his future lay on the track. It was unusual for an athlete of such prodigious talent to be discovered so late, but Adam Monaghan was not a run-of-the-mill athlete.

Born and raised in rural Oxfordshire to wealthy parents of Irish descent, he'd shown no early signs of athletic ability. He'd been a normal kid. Intelligent, a little introverted, keen to please. He enjoyed a kick-about with friends, loved a game of tennis in the summer, but all to no great effect.

It was only when his parents sent him to boarding school at the age of eleven that his athletic skills became apparent. Trials for rugby and cricket came and went. Adam wasn't disappointed when not selected. He'd only entered the trials to keep up with his friends. He had no desire to participate in team sport. Besides, deep down, he knew he wasn't good enough.

But at cross-country, he excelled.

He would leave his classmates far behind. He didn't particularly push himself; it just came naturally. Adam's enjoyment came from escaping the confines of the school, plush though it was, and getting back to the countryside he'd been brought up in, rather than in the sport itself.

Selection for the county followed, but without real success. Adam had little competitiveness in him. His opponents had less ability but greater desire. He won a few medals but nothing to match the results his ability merited.

At the age of fourteen, he dropped out of the athletics club altogether to concentrate on academia. A wise choice. His results were outstanding. He took GCSEs a year early, all A*, so Adam was a year ahead of his fellow schoolmates. It meant he had time on his hands. He went back to running. Not as part of a club, just on the roads and fields surrounding the school.

Whilst in sixth form, boredom set in. The school timetable set aside many free periods for study. Adam's natural intelligence meant he had little need for them. He had too much free time, especially on Tuesday's when he had only two lessons to attend.

Fate decreed that it was a Tuesday on which the PE department invited Noah Odago, a former member of Team GB, into school to give a motivational speech.

Afterwards, Odago challenged students to a series of races on the school's athletics track. He gave all-comers a hundred metres start over a four-hundred metre track. He beat them all.

Adam had wandered across. The final group of eight athletes were lined up ready to go, Odago behind them. A PE teacher, Mr Franklin, had a quiet word in the athlete's ear. Noah looked across at Adam and beckoned him to join the others.

Adam pointed a finger at his chest. 'Me?', it asked. Odago nodded so, in jeans and sweatshirt, Adam lined up on the track.

Mr Franklin waved them off. The ex-international athlete waited until the group entered the first bend then set off in pursuit. By the time they hit the second bend, Odago had caught them all. All except Adam, who remained thirty paces ahead.

Odago was still in pursuit when Adam crossed the finishing line. Adam didn't stop. He carried on for a second circuit.

Odago closed the gap but still trailed by almost twenty metres as Adam crossed the line and set off on a third lap. Odago didn't follow. Instead, he stood on the finishing line and studied the prodigy as Adam powered on with little loss of form throughout his third circuit.

Noah Odago applauded him home.

Adam crouched on the track, sucking air into his lungs. Odago wandered over and stretched out an arm, hauling him to his feet.

"'Ow do". The thick inflection in Noah's voice placed him firmly in the West Midlands. "Respect, man. Who you represent?"

It took Adam a moment to decipher the accent. He offered an apologetic smile. "No-one. Just a hobby".

"No, come on, man. I mean it. Which club you with?".

"I'm not. Was in the school's until about three years ago but nothing before or since".

"That were seriously bostin', that were". Adam looked confused. "It was very good", Odago translated.

"Thanks", a sheepish grin on Adam's face.

"You must run somewhere, though. Can't just walk onto a track and blow the pants off me like that."

"Just around the school grounds. Sometimes along Fairweather Road and onto Addler's Farm."

"I meant which track."

"Oh. No track. There's no fun running around a track like a hamster in a wheel."

"Well you should do, then."

"Nope. Not interested."

"Come on, man. Let's talk about this. I've never seen anyone do what you just did. You don't know how good you are. I reckon you could go all the way with a bit of coaching".

Adam flushed and laughed. He'd never been good at taking compliments. Noah ignored the awkwardness and continued.

"Y'am bin serious, y'am bin, man".

Adam shrugged his shoulders. Looked at the athlete blankly. Shook his head. "Nope. Didn't get that."

"I-am-being-serious-I-really-am", Noah translated with exaggerated deliberation.

Adam laughed again before Noah put his arm around him and led him away, keen to learn more about this burgeoning talent.

By the time Noah had bid a perplexed Adam "Tarra-a bit" at the end of the afternoon, Adam had his first coach. Noah Odago.

The relationship hadn't been smooth. Odago was frustrated by Adam's refusal to practice on the track. Adam insisted that it be done his way or not at all; he wasn't sufficiently in love with the sport to do something he disliked.

The professional in Odago admired the young man's principles as much as his talent so he'd agreed to Adam's methods, on the proviso that he entered athletics events Odago recommended. Adam did. And won most of them.

Ultimately, less than four years later, those events included the Commonwealth Games 5,000 metres trial. Adam didn't win his heat but did enough to qualify for the final as one of three fastest losers. In the final, he came alive.

He led at the bell before showing his inexperience. He left a gap on the inside through which two athletes squeezed. Adam Monaghan trailed off third behind Marc Smith and Geoff Chambers but he'd finished comfortably within the qualifying time. He'd done enough to make the provisional squad alongside Smith, Chambers, and a fourth athlete; Roderick Best., a veteran.

With only two places on the team up for grabs, and with Geoff Chambers just recovered from injury, today was the day Adam would discover if the England team's selection panel were prepared to take a punt on him.

He'd know by the time he'd finished his training run. He hoped not to have a decision to make. He'd already been accepted by Harvard to do post-graduate research. Not to mention the lucrative offer of employment with a major motor company based in Sunderland, subject to obtaining a first in his finals.

His finals... sod's law that, just like buses coming two at once, he was also due to receive confirmation of his degree today. Adam brushed such thoughts aside as he kicked on with his training run and the University campus faded into the distance behind him.

Habit told him that there would be no traffic on the quiet streets around the cathedral but he still glanced both ways before he upped his pace and powered across it.

He settled back into a rhythmic stride pattern as he traversed the ancient courtyard in front of the cathedral. The route was familiar to him; familiarity brought a welcome sense of comfort to him, today of all days. He was nervous. Nagging doubts surfaced. Doubts he put to one side as he continued his run.

He swept down the narrow arc of Canal Hill, shortening his stride as the downhill gradient increased. He stepped off the kerb as he passed the Longboat Inn. The landlord was already busy littering the path with wicker tables and chairs.

It was here that Adam had first met her, and he knew this was the first of countless reminders of her. He shook his head to remove beads of sweat, not to mention more doubts.

The summer cold he'd harboured for weeks caused him to run the back of his hand across his nose. He sniffed and spat the mucus into the gutter before it could clog his throat.

At the foot of the hill, he sprinted along the towpath until he reached the willow-shaded hollow where they had first made love one balmy summer's eve. From here, he veered sharp left onto the ancient stone bridge – the humpbacked dowager of the canal – on which he had proposed and, to his delight and astonishment, she had accepted.

He changed his breathing pattern when he reached the far side of the canal. He breathed in through his nose, held the oxygen in his lungs for a second longer before he exhaled, shooting the spent air out of his mouth with a violent push which puffed his cheeks.

His feet sought out the comfort of the lush grass alongside the towpath. Noah frowned upon him running on anything other than hard surfaces but the pavement had crumbled away; an accident waiting to happen. He couldn't afford that. Not this close to the Games. This cold was bad enough but it would pass. An ankle ligament injury wouldn't.

His mind flipped back to the e-mails awaiting him. He would know soon enough if he'd been selected. He didn't want his thoughts to continue along those lines so it was a relief when he came across the ramshackle bungalow they were to renovate together, something he'd promised to tackle just as soon as he knew the outcome.

Adam's thighs and calves began to tighten, a consequence of lactic acid accumulating in his muscles. He shortened his stride to compensate and headed towards the dank underpass that cut beneath the canal and under both the busy by-pass and mainline railway running parallel to it.

He signalled a 'No thank you' to the Big Issue seller at the subway entrance and splashed through puddles he hoped were of water and not the product of the Big Issue seller's bladder.

Midway through the tunnel, phlegm caught in the back of his palette and he coughed violently. It echoed like a rifle retort, startling an elderly woman who shortened the leash on two tan-and-white terriers as they jumped and yapped at the passing athlete. Adam nodded an acknowledgement to her then flattened himself against the subway wall to avoid a cyclist who careered into view at the exit.

Adam emerged into bright sunlight. Although temporarily blinded, he lowered his head in preparation for the tortuous uphill grind rather than as a means of protecting his eyes.

Puffing more heavily, he began the most difficult part of his daily run: the steep incline. The route wasn't known as the 'Vicious Circle' for nothing. It provided a better aerobic workout than any gym could offer.

The blue 'Hospital' direction indicator pointing up a sheer bank of steps off to his left brought an ironic smile to his face. It was here he'd undergone his medical not two weeks ago. What a futile exercise that was, he thought. He glanced at the stopwatch on his wrist. It told him he was on course for a personal best. Medical was a formality if he could run the Circle in this time.

Still, they'd insisted on it. And, still, he worried about it. A shudder caught him by surprise. Brought his mind back onto the run.

This was the toughest part of the course; the steepest part of the climb. He pumped his arms to provide leverage and it was a relief when he browed the summit and saw the stone walls of the University, the modern tower blocks of the distant city centre a world away.

The road was busier now. He had to run on the spot at the crossing whilst waiting for a gap in the traffic. Adam nipped the bridge of his nose between his fingers and blew away the mucus lining his nasal cavity.

A mother with a toddler restrained her child from stepping into the road when Adam sprinted across whilst still under the orders of the red man. She mumbled something about setting a bad example and he waved an apologetic acknowledgement to her.

Another glance at the stopwatch told him he'd made up even more time. He was reaching his peak in time for the Games just as Noah had predicted.

Almost home now. Just the University Great Hall to skirt then he could shower and relax.

And check his e-mails.

All three of them.

GWEN

'I was working as a waitress in a cocktail bar'.

Gwen always quoted the Human League song when friends asked how she met him. In fact, she was collecting glasses from sodden tables on the sticky-floored Longboat Inn but that didn't sound half as glamorous.

His glass wasn't quite empty when she picked it up but he hadn't complained. Not like any of the other students. That's what had first appealed to her about him. He'd noticed her mistake, she could tell in his eyes, but he didn't embarrass her. Quiet and thoughtful. She liked that.

Gwen also liked his eyes, the shock of unruly dark hair, and his shy smile. Not to mention his guns. He was lean but taught, with well-defined musculature beneath the sleeveless vest he wore.

She'd made the running – an ironic turn of phrase once she'd got to know him – when he returned to the inn a couple of days later. He was a bit sweaty on that occasion, she'd thought, but in an attractive musky way.

What had particularly endeared her to him was that he wasn't 'obvious'. In fact, quite the opposite. She noticed a bit of a rash on his arm and had made it an excuse to make bodily contact with him. "Ooh. What you done to your arm?", she asked.

When she stroked it, he'd jumped away from her as if she'd run a charge of electricity through him. 'How cute', she'd thought.

"That? Not sure. Had it for a while now. Probably just eczema. Maybe a bit of stress. Exams, and that".

"Let me see", Gwen asked. She took his wrist and turned his arm, stroking the red patch of skin. Her tactic worked. He'd slipped his hand into hers, let her stroke his arm. He'd run his fingers through her hair. Then they kissed, and it was Gwen's turn to feel the electricity.

They exchanged numbers, began dating (again, she'd initiated the contact), and were soon in love.

Twelve months on, he'd dropped to one knee in the middle of a bridge over the canal, blocking the passage of numerous passers-by, and asked her to marry him. He'd become embarrassed when the folk lining the bridge hooted and clapped when she'd said yes.

Gwen always smiled to herself whenever the memory came to her, which was often. She was astonished when he was astonished she'd accepted. Adam had told her that their relationship had to be kept low profile while he was training and studying. He didn't want outside influences to affect either, so she was shocked when the proposal came.

She found it difficult to accept that he still didn't want to go public with their families even after their engagement, though.

"Come on, Adam. Let me tell my parents. They'd love you, you know. No need to be shy".

"No, Gwen. I'm serious. I can't let things detract me from my studies. Every holiday it'd be, like, 'Oh why don't you and Adam come down?' Then it would soon be every weekend. And I need to study. Yeah, I need to train too, but I've got to get this degree. And a first at that".

"You know, I'm beginning to think you're ashamed of me. At least let me tell my sister. We share everything. She'll know something's up".

Adam frowned. "It's still a no, Gwendoline. Friends know because they see us here. We can't avoid that. Besides, I need to be close to Noah for my training. I can't go running off at a whim. If you're honest with yourself, your parents would want you to spend time there with me, wouldn't they?".

She knew it made sense, some of it. But it still hurt. And she told him so. "Adam, I can't pretend that I'm happy with this. I'm not buying into this Noah business. He rarely sees you anyway. But I appreciate you need your study time to compensate for the hours you lose when you're running. But, please, think about it. For my sake, yeah?".

"I will. Think about it, that is. But you think about something too, will you? If I do make it as an athlete – and if I decide I want to – you think about whether you're ready for press intrusion. Poking their nose into past relationships. Looking for anything murky. Whether you're ready for TV cameras. For people asking for autographs. Treating you as if you're not there. Because that will happen. And you know what – that's what I'm dreading".

"You do know you're not a member of One Direction, don't you?", Gwen smiled, then instantly regretted it when she saw his eyes had filled with tears.

Gwen took his hand in both of hers. "Honey", she said, "I'd never thought how hard it was for you. I'm sorry. I know how private you are. Let's carry on as we are. I won't mention it again. I promise. When you are ready, though. Tell me."

He nodded and forced a smile.

Gwen remained in hope. Hope and denial. Now, very soon, possibly even today, she could tell her parents and sister. She was marrying Adam Monaghan, the athlete.

Unless, of course, he chose to leave the spotlight behind and take the Harvard offer without her. Even worse, he might choose Sunderland. With her.

With Adam, anything was possible.

MARIE

Marie stirred the few prawns left on the barbecue. She checked the temperature of the embers, hovered her hand above the grill tray, and snatched her hand away as the hairs on the back of it began to singe. Just enough heat to let the shellfish sing, she concluded.

Whilst she waited for the food to cook, she popped the tab on a can of lager and gulped the contents down as if she were a ranch-hand in the outback. She flopped back onto her lounger. Sunlight caught the pool, and her natural tan was exaggerated by the ruby and gold shades reflected upon her.

The chirrup of crickets offered a musical accompaniment to the food sizzling on the barbeque. Not even out of winter and the temperature already twenty-three. Did she miss home? That'll be a 'no'.

Summer would be fading to autumn back home. There'd be drizzle in the air, the wind cool. Jumpers would be coming out the closet. That's how she imagined it, anyway, and it enticed a laugh out of her.

"Something funny?", asked a voice alongside her.

"No. Just thinking. About home".

"Home's a long way away".

"It is". She reached over and rubbed the chest of the man alongside her. "But I feel perfectly at home here, Scott. With you".

"Whoa. You'll be asking to have my children next. Steady on, girl". He tilted his head and winked at her.

"I think not", she replied, trailing her fingers down to the waistband of his jeans. "My children will have better genes than yours".

He feigned a groan at her joke before leaning across to kiss her.

"Those prawns done yet?".

"Oh how romantic. Trust you to break the moment". Marie laughed again. "Anyway, isn't the man supposed to be the one in charge of the barbie?"

"He is. I am. I'm telling you to do it. That's being in charge, isn't it?".

She made to get up from her lounger.

"And while you're up", he added, "Get me another beer, will you?"

They both laughed as he dodged the can she flung at him.

Marie sensed movement behind her. She saw nothing at first then heard a noise overhead. A splash of colour in the periphery of her vision caught her attention. She looked up to see a bird, plumage as lurid as a carnival float, resting atop the mesh net encasing the pool.

Marie stared in wonder. As if bashful at the attention, the parakeet raised a wing and tucked its head beneath it.

"Rainbow lorikeet", Scott informed her. "A local one at that."

"How'd you know?"

"What? That it's local? Notice the yellow band of feathers it's plucking at under its wing? Well, only Queensland lorikeets have them".

Marie looked at Scott. "You know so much. Will you teach me?"

He snorted a laugh. "I will, but before you move onto birds you need to learn how to recognise the spiders. It's a bit more important out here".

She became serious for a moment. "You know, coming here was the best thing I could have done. Didn't intend staying in Oz this long. You're the one to blame for that. But, I kinda' do miss home. At least,

I miss my folks. And I worry about Gwen".

"Worry about her? Why? I know you two are close but from what you told me you never saw that much of each other".

"I know. But I just get the feeling that she's keeping something from me. She used to post all sorts on Facebook but over the last few months there's been very little".

"Maybe she's run off with David Beckham".

"No, Scott. I'm being serious. She used stick photos of her blokes on her Facebook wall all the time, usually with saucy comments. Now everything's so.. I don't know. So solemn, I guess. Not spontaneous".

"Perhaps she really has run off with David Beckham, then".

"You cannot be serious", she scolded in a fake John McEnroe accent. "Not for a minute, can you?"

"Yes I can. I'm serious about you. Let's leave the food. It's nice and cool inside. In the bedroom…"

ADAM

The University was deserted. Always was during recess. Adam had to seek special dispensation to remain there so he was close to Noah Odago. Not that it mattered. Adam's training routine was so unconventional Noah left him to it, in the main. Gwen was right about that.

The University had consented to his request immediately, foreseeing the publicity and kudos that came with housing a member of England's Commonwealth Games team.

He didn't have the heart to tell them his selection was far from a formality. For a number of reasons.

The oak-panelled corridor was haunted by his rasping breath as he fumbled for his key. His faded blue singlet, stained black with sweat, leeched to his damp shoulders. Adam stood for a moment, bent double, hands on hips, before he turned the key and entered the cluttered room.

Showing admirable restraint, Adam walked past the computer terminal and made for the kitchen. He poured himself an orange juice, downed it in one, and reached for an energy drink.

Adam hesitated, put the can back in the fridge, and switched on the PC. He towelled himself down, the fibres irritating the rash on his arm, while it booted up. The screen illuminated, revealing a photograph of the love of his life.

He pressed a random key to expose the password screen and typed in the eight secret digits. He was stripped and in the shower even before the list of e-mails appeared.

Refreshed, with the towel now wrapped around his mid-riff, Adam sat on the edge of the bed and stared at the screen. Seven new e-mails.

One was from Noah. He'd check that later. Another two were from on-line discount voucher companies. He immediately deleted one, the title making it clear it was for beauty treatments, without opening it and left the other, a bargain weekend break in London, for later consideration. He'd already deleted the e-mail offering him cheap Viagra.

That left him with three. He scratched his arm and noticed he'd ruptured the surface while he pondered which e-mail to open first: his final degree results, or either of the ones from the Commonwealth Games Committee. After a moment that seemed like a lifetime, he clicked on the envelope alongside one of the messages.

He gave the contents a superficial glance before closing the mail. The cursor hovered between the other two as Adam pondered which to open. It was a pointless exercise. He knew which one had to be first.

Adam felt his finger tremble as it floated above the mouse. After a brief pause, a sneeze, and a deep intake of breath, he depressed the button.

It was a few moments more before he forced himself to look at the screen.

"Shit".

He gathered his thoughts. Tried to compose himself. He knew what this meant. For him, and for them. He had to tell her.

He coughed, reached for his phone, and speed-dialled the number.

Adam prayed she wouldn't answer.

She did.

"Gwen? Adam. Hi. Listen. It's not good news".

GWEN

"Oh. Right. Right. Thanks for letting me know". Her voice sounded detached. She FELT detached, as if she were watching her own actions being orchestrated by an unseen puppeteer.

She could scarcely accept the news she'd just heard. She leant forward and tenderly ran a finger around the oval frame which housed the photograph of her and Adam smiling into each other's eyes rather than the camera lens.

"Poor Adam", she whispered to his photograph. She knew what it meant to him. 'Poor Adam? Poor ME', she thought.

Secretly, she'd loved the thought of being with an athletics star. The WAG status it would defer on her. Now, all that was changed. Where once, only a phone call ago, they'd had a future together, now she wondered if they had a future apart.

Gwen tried to tell herself it wasn't the end of the world. That there was still a chance; still a hope for the future. But in her mind the first domino had been toppled and her cherished dreams were tumbling around her.

She was alone and insecure. Frightened to think of the future. Needed to talk. As usual, she turned to Marie. Her sister may have been a couple of years younger, may be in Australia, but she always seemed to know the right things to say. And Gwen needed Marie to say the right thing now more than ever before.

Theirs had never been one of those relationships where they needed to be together to prove the bond between them. That was what had made her emigration easier to take. Indeed, they'd seldom seen much of each other even before Marie's gap year had turned into something more permanent.

But Gwen knew Marie would help. Her sister had never met

Adam, hadn't even seen a photograph of him. Thanks to his pig-headedness, she didn't know of his ambitions. Didn't even know he existed in her life.

She thought all that would change once the selection process was over. Over? This would never be over.

Gwen shed a quiet tear. Drank a glass of water to calm down. Then she dialled Marie.

No answer.

She checked the time difference. Ten hours shouldn't be a problem, so dialled again.

Let it ring.

"Come on, Marie. I need you".

And ring.

"Damn", Gwen exclaimed. She remembered the new boyfriend. An English lad she'd met on her travels. Now staying near her in Brisbane. That's where she'd be.

But Gwen still needed to talk. She had a leaflet somewhere. Finally found it tucked inside a Chinese take-away menu. She took a deep breath and dialled.

"Hello. How can we help you?", asked a gentle, soothing male voice at the end of the line.

Gwen found herself pouring out the full story, all her hopes and fears, hesitating only when she told the anonymous voice how selfish she felt, but needing to know what it all meant for her.

She found no comfort in his reply.

MARIE

God, she felt good. She stretched herself as lazily as the kitten left behind in her apartment. Would have purred like her, too, had she been able.

Marie gathered the sheet around her nakedness toga-fashion, and giggled. She'd always thought the male physique looked faintly ridiculous and, whilst Scott had looked – and felt – terrific last night, the slumbering figure spread-eagled on the bed alongside her now merely confirmed her original opinion.

After showering, she sat on the edge of the bed to dress. As she cupped herself into her brassiere and fastened it behind her, she bent to pick up the photograph album they had discarded the night before.

She smiled at seven-year-old Scott on his bike, laughed at the longhaired sixteen-year-old. The naked twenty-four-year-old stirred beside her.

"Hmm. Morning", he yawned. His jaw made a noise like sandpaper as he scratched at its bristles.

"Morning", she smiled back.

"God, you're beautiful".

"God, you're ugly!" They laughed. Kissed.

She turned a couple of pages in the album as he curled against her.

"Where's this?" she asked pointing to a picture of Scott and a friend with four bikinied girls. He peered around her elbow. "Cap Ferat. France. About three years ago".

"She's pretty", said Marie, indicating one of the girls.

"Not bad", he said, disinterest in his voice. "Trudi, I think"..

"And her?"

"Joan. Or June. Something like that. "Hey – you're jealous".

"No I'm not", she said. 'Yes I am', she thought, wondering if they were better lovers than she.

She moved her finger along the photo. "What about this one?"

"Look, I can't even remember her name. Nothing happened. They were just some girls we bumped into".

"Really honestly?"

"Really honestly. Now can we forget it? Please?"

"Ok, ok", she smiled.

"Good. Now get those clothes off again!"

"Oh, I love it when you're masterful", she mocked. She unclasped her bra and waved it like a white lace flag in surrender. As Marie rolled astride him, he waggled a finger in the direction of the photograph.

"Actually, I lied. I did have a mad, passionate affair with one".

For a moment, Marie froze. Her gaze followed the path of his finger. And she collapsed in a fit of giggles.

"Oh you. You're impossible!" she laughed.

But Scott was only smiling; smiling at fond memories. Not at memories of four bikinied girls, but at memories of someone else in the photograph.

Memories of dear, gorgeous Adam.

BOOK THREE

BRITTLE JUSTICE

AUTHOR'S NOTE

Everyone's mother is their inspiration. Mine was – is – no different. She always championed my cause, offered me sage advice, and encouraged me in everything I did.

Mam was so proud when work attributed to me first appeared in a sports magazine then, later, national newspapers and travel guides. Sadly, she passed away in September 2014 after a sound innings of 86. She never lived to see any of my fiction hit print.

Recently, I revisited some of the papers that she'd accumulated over the years. Amongst articles she'd typed up for the Church magazine on her aged typewriter, I came across a 500-word short story she'd written. It was about a young man being tried for a crime he didn't commit. She called it 'Trial and Tribulation'.

I don't know why or when she wrote it but I read it with a tear in my eye, never having realized that I'd moved her to try her own hand at writing.

I took it upon myself to take her original idea and use it as a basis for something a little lengthier. So, in homage to Mam, here is her 'Trial and Tribulation', presented to you as 'Brittle Justice'.

If you enjoy reading it half as much as I enjoyed writing it, she'd have been very proud.

CHAPTER ONE

1st November 1965

A thin waft of watery sunlight filtered through the high window. I felt it play on my face like fingers plucking at a harp as I stirred from an uneasy sleep. I slowly opened my eyes and took momentary pleasure from the warmth of the sun. Then full consciousness returned and I was filled with a familiar dark sense of despair. I realised where I was.

My joints ached from the confines of my narrow bunk. My skin itched from the course blanket which covered my body. And my soul cried out in pain just as it had every morning for the past few months.

I turned on my back, reached for the cigarettes at my side, and lit up. I inhaled and slowly blew out a cloud of blue / grey smoke. I watched it slowly filter upwards, imagining shapes and stories within it, before it merged with the grey walls of my prison cell.

Three weeks had passed since my trial for murder had begun. Murder. Me; Jimmy Finlay. I ask you. The closer the end of the trial approached, the more my angst had grown. Until today. Today, I would hear the closing speeches. The judge would sum up and the jury would retire. Just one more day, I told myself.

One more day; or the rest of my life.

A forlorn hopelessness reached into my innards. It grasped and twisted. Hard. On the facts before the jury, how could they find me anything but guilty? As each day went by, even I began to doubt my innocence such is the weight of evidence against me.

But innocent I am. That's why I'm so angry, and that's why my brief had warned me that I risked a contempt charge if I were to vent my spleen in the dock. Why he had advised me not to take the stand.

He had done his best, my barrister had. He'd stressed my unblemished character, my good nature. He'd dredged up a whole litany of people who I thought hardly knew me. They all sung my praises. 'Charitable individual'. 'Never an ounce of trouble'. Even the old 'pillar of the community' line had been trotted out.

But that's all I had in my favour. Character references versus indisputable facts. Except they weren't facts, were they?

Every day, I watched the jurors faces, paying more attention to their reactions than listening to the evidence. My future was in their hands: two housewives, a secretary, a schoolmistress, an architect, a builder, a postman, two clerks, two factory workers and an unemployed man who looked like a murderer if ever anyone did; twelve strangers whose faces I had come to know as well as my own.

I'd willed myself to gauge their thoughts, to look for a glimmer of hope. I found none. All were inscrutable. Even the 'murderer'.

Footsteps echoed in the corridor outside, cold and forbidding. The rattle of keys, like the chains of Jacob Marley's ghost, reached my ears. The cell door opened and the guard stood in the doorway. He laid a flimsy tin tray on the floor and exited. No words. Just a smirk.

I looked at the tray. A cup of murky water that was supposed to be tea, and a bowl of something that looked like wallpaper paste. At least they paid me the courtesy of leaving a newspaper. I had no interest in it. Ironic, really. I wouldn't be here if it hadn't been for a newspaper.

I took a deep draw on my cigarette, rested my head on the rock of a pillow, and relived the events that had led to me being in this impossible position.

CHAPTER TWO

The day had started ordinarily enough. I prepared my usual solitary breakfast of jam on toast and a cup of Earl Grey before setting out early. I'm an Auctioneer's Clerk in the City Centre, you see, and I have to rise early in order to cover the distance. I don't drive.

I'm not normally the only one up, though, and that day was no exception. Arnold, the old man who ran the Newsagents on the corner, was opening up. I couldn't call Arnold a friend. I hardly knew him. But over the two years I've lived there I suppose we've developed a kind of comradeship.

As well as being the only ones awake in the neighbourhood, old Arnold had an interest in antiques and I often picked up small items for him at the various auctions I attended. We had the same routine each day. I would buy a pack of Player's No. 6 – Arnold introduced me to them when they came out a few months ago – and collect my morning newspaper.

On my return, I'd buy the evening paper which Arnold always kept back for me. I'm sure the old man waited for my visit because I always heard the clock of the bolt and the rattle of the door sign turning from 'Open' to 'Closed' as he shut the door behind me.

Arnold was a lonely old soul. He once told me his wife had passed away during the War and he had no other family. I think he looked forward to my visits though I'm not arrogant enough to believe he thought of me as family.

I remember he showed me a faded black and white photograph of his wife. Norma, she was called if I remember correctly. Arnold always dressed impeccably in suit, bow tie and waistcoat; an ornately carved walking stick by his side. A real gent, he was. He constantly had a battered old pocket watch attached to his waistcoat. When he took the watch from his pocket and opened the case to show me, Norma's photograph had been cut so it fit inside nice and snug.

I recall a scrap of paper or something had fluttered to the floor when he showed me her picture. Neither of us had noticed but another customer did and he retrieved it for Arnold who gratefully replaced the object – I think it was probably a postage stamp – into the watch. Arnold had given the man a quarter of boiled sweets as a thank you. Typical of Arnold, that was. Courteous as ever.

Anyway, the day before my life changed for ever, I reminded Arnold that I planned to attend an auction the next day rather than spend it in the office. I'd shown Arnold the catalogue a couple of days earlier so he could see if anything caught his eye. When I called for my evening paper, the old man told me he was interested in an ornate snuff box.

He asked me what I thought it was worth. I told him the lot estimate was £70 but I'd be surprised if it fetched so much. The old man shuffled his way to the till and took out a crisp, new £50 note. "Anything up to this, you get it for me, young man", he'd said to me.

As he passed me the note, he caught his hand on a jagged piece of glass on the showcase. It was a nasty cut so I quickly wrapped a handkerchief around the gash to stem the flow of blood. He was so grateful for my help, bless him. I turned down his offer of a quarter of Candy Shrimps, though.

So, the next day; THE day. I almost forgot I wasn't going into the office. It would take me a little longer to get to the auction rooms. A glance at the clock told me I was running late so I gulped down my tea and left most of the breakfast.

I'd still make time to pop into Arnold's for my paper and cigarettes, though. Couldn't disappoint the old boy. Besides, I wanted to reassure him that I hadn't forgotten his instruction to bid on the snuff box. I'd already decided I'd go as high as the £70 estimate if necessary. I'd make it up with £20 of my own money. It wouldn't be the first time I'd done it but there was no need for him to know, was there?

It was a dank and grey morning. The weather had forgot it was summer. Puffs of steam and smoke billowed from teetering chimney stacks, creating a thick haze that made it difficult to see the sky above.

In the lamplight, ghost-like shadows spread across the pavement, miserable silhouettes in the gloom of a fateful day.

One of the shadows was that of a man emerging from Arnold's shop. I remember my feeling of disappointment when I saw him. I recall thinking it wasn't right; that it was my job to be the first to greet him each day. Strange how we become fixated on our daily routine, isn't it? Anyway, I digress. The spectre turned into something more substantial as the man scuttled past me before he merged into greyness and disappeared around the corner.

I turned up the collar on my coat and reached into the pocket for my cigarettes. Of course, I'd run out. Just another reason for destiny and fate to whisper their conspiracies against me; another reason to ensure I didn't bypass the newsagents.

Head down, I hurried towards the shop. I always whistle or hum when I go into Arnold's just so I don't startle the old man. The door has a bell that jingles when it's opened but that could be anyone entering, couldn't it?

So, giving it my best rendition of 'King of the Road', I pushed open the door. I'd just got to the line about "Ain't got no cigarettes' when I saw him. Poor Arnold. On the floor. Blood pooling all around him.

I was transfixed. I remember the first thing that sprung into my mind was a quote from Macbeth. *"Who would have thought the old man to have so much blood in him?"*

Then adrenalin kicked in and I rushed to Arnold. I slipped on the river of blood and banged my head on the shop counter as I stumbled in my rush to aid him. He lay still, his walking stick across his chest. I threw it off him. It was then I saw the knife buried deep within him.

I pulled the knife from his body, careful not to cause more damage, but it was useless. Gentle, kind Arnold was already dead.

As I knelt beside the body, I saw the blood on my trousers. In a panic, I realised the implications. I became breathless. I thought I was going to pass out as my sight faded. Then I realised my sight had diminished because a shadow had cast over me.

I turned around to see what had caused the shadow. And that was when I saw the policeman, who had chosen that moment to enter the shop, standing in the doorway.

I knew that he, too, realised the implications. And another line from Macbeth sprung unbidden.

"Is this a dagger which I see before me, the handle towards my hand?"

CHAPTER THREE

So that's how I came to be here; waiting to be shunted off to the final day of my trial. When they came to take me, the newspaper still lay where the guard had left it, rolled so tightly he could have used it as his truncheon. The breakfast tray sat alongside, the contents untouched.

This would be the last day I'd be ferried in the back of a black Maria like sheep to slaughter. I remember nothing of the journey. My mind had shut down. It only sparked into life when I was back standing in the dock, flanked by two policemen on either side of me.

I snapped out of the trance-like state I'd forced myself into. I looked around. My barrister, a lean man in his late-thirties by the name of Angus Simmons, acknowledged me with a brief nod of the head. I tried to smile back but my mouth wouldn't respond.

The courtroom was full, every ancient wooden pew taken. The press gallery overflowed. The jurors sat to my front and left on a slightly raised gantry. One of the women offered me a sheepish smile. I was grateful for it. I somehow managed to return her smile. I needed all the help I could get. The other jurors stared straight ahead.

"All rise".

I had come to dread hearing those words every day. My stomach lurched and rumbled, the noise masked by the shuffling of feet and general hub-bub as the judge entered his courtroom.

Justice Maxwell Yeo-Carter was impossibly old, thin and gaunt. His wig, grander than any other in the courtroom, sat atop his head like a kitchen mop. He took his seat on a platform in front of the Royal Coat of Arms, and the hullaballoo repeated itself as the public gallery settled.

The stenographer in front of the bench pulled on her fingers to relax them. The crack of her knuckles made me squirm. It's the little things like that which will stay with me.

Justice Yeo-Carter's opening remarks passed me by. My legal team had told me that what was said today would determine the outcome. I didn't like the way they said 'the' outcome. It was 'my' outcome. I wanted them to know it mattered to ME.

The prosecution barrister was a tiny man called Lawrence Boythorn. I assumed he'd been named after the character in Bleak House. He certainly looked as if he'd stepped straight from the pages of a Dickensian novel.

Boythorn pulled himself up to his full five foot four inches, tucked his thumbs into his gown, and began his closing address.

"My Lord", he paused and made a deferential bow towards the judge, "ladies and gentlemen of the jury". He paused again. "I shall be brief".

That was a relief.

"I remind you that you must judge this case on the facts before you. You need to be satisfied 'beyond all reasonable doubt' that the facts prove that this man – James Joseph Finlay – murdered Arnold Cooper, a frail, defenceless shopkeeper".

He paused again for effect. The gallery was silent as a grave, all hanging on his every word.

"I will be brief for one very simple reason: I contend that you can reach no verdict other than 'guilty'. The facts are indisputable".

He looked at me. I returned his gaze, not wanting to indicate guilt by looking away. It was difficult for me. I'm not comfortable with eye-contact. Makes me uneasy. It worked this time, though, because Boythorn turned away from me. Turned to face the jury, and strolled towards them.

"The defendant admits to being in the newsagents where Mr Cooper was found dead, savagely murdered. Fact. You have heard the undisputed testimony from PC Thwaites – a fine, upstanding police officer – that the accused was discovered kneeling over the body of Mr Cooper. Fact. The defendant had on his person a handkerchief stained with the blood of Mr Cooper. Fact. The defendant's finger prints were found on the handle of the knife used to kill the victim. Fact. And in his possession was a £50 note which also contained traces of Mr Cooper's blood. Fact".

I looked at the jury, disturbed to see many of them nodding in agreement. I shifted my gaze to my legal team. Angus Simmons sat impassive. Impossible for me to read whether he was as well prepared for his – my – opportunity to present my case.

Boythorn wasn't finished yet, though.

"You have heard testimony", he continued, "from Mr Richard Moor of Midland Bank. Mr Moor has confirmed that the serial number of said £50 note was amongst those handed to the victim the day before the crime. Fact. And, if that wasn't already enough, you have heard medical evidence to indicate that a bruise sustained on the forehead of the accused is consistent with receiving a blow from a wooden implement. In other words, from the walking stick of Arnold Cooper as he fought bravely for his life. F-A-C-T fact."

He's good at his job, this Boythorn bloke, I thought. I'd resigned myself to the verdict. My team would have to be on their mettle if I stood any chance. Then it got even worse for me.

Boythorn prowled back and forth in front of the jury as if he were a caged lion. All eyes were on him. Several jurors took notes.

"Now", he continued, "The defence will no doubt tell you that the defendant has no previous criminal record".

Another pause.

"Well, neither had Dr Crippen".

Laughter.

"During the course of this trial, the defence has paraded in front of you a stream of witnesses who haven't witnessed anything at all. All they've done is tell you what a good man the defendant is".

He turned from the jury and walked up to me in the dock.

"Well, m'lord and ladies and gentlemen of the jury, Mr Arnold Cooper also thought the defendant was a 'good man'. And look where that led him".

The barrister swished his cloak around like a pantomime villain. He walked briskly to the jury. "But remember you are judging this case on facts, facts, facts".

He banged his fist on the wooden jury box with each 'fact'.

"And I put it to you that the facts can lead you to only one conclusion". He turned and pointed to me with outstretched arm. "The conclusion that James Joseph Finlay is guilty of murder".

He turned triumphantly to Justice Yeo-Carter. "My lord. Once these twelve good men – and women – have reached the only verdict upon which they reasonably can, I ask that you view this crime as one most heinous. As such, if it would please the court, I ask that you confer upon the accused the maximum possible sentence within your powers".

I almost expected him to bow to the gallery as he retook his seat.

I glanced at my brief. He looked pale. I'd seen him exchange words with the rest of our team during the prosecution's summing-up at the point where he'd ridiculed the only defence I had: my good character. I knew then that he'd given up on me.

"Mr. Simmons. Would you care to sum up the case for the defence, please?"

My barrister finished scribbling a few last-minute notes before rising to his feet. He cleared his throat before opening with the words "My lord, ladies and mental men of the jury".

The gallery laughed. Boythorn and company put their heads down and sniggered.

"Mr Simmons. Perhaps you would care to go out and come back in again?", Justice Yeo-Carter offered. Not the most auspicious of starts.

He began again.

"Yes, m'lud. Sorry m'lud. Members of the jury. Please, take a look at the man before you". He stepped aside so the jurors could see me. As if they hadn't seen enough of me already.

"The prosecution has painted a picture of Mr Finlay as a ruthless, violent, man. A man who would take the life of a frail pensioner he had befriended. Go on, take a good look", he invited.

Simmons had briefed me in advance. He'd stressed the importance of looking the jurors in the eye at this point. I tried, I really did, but the only one I could look at was the lady who had smiled at me.

"Does this look the kind of man who would take a life in cold blood? The prosecution has ridiculed witnesses who have come forward, under oath, may I remind you, to vouch for Mr Finlay's kindly nature. Can they all be wrong? Can so many have misjudged the character of this innocent man?"

He moved closer to the jury. He looked at each one in turn.

"Remember that you must be certain beyond all reasonable doubt – CERTAIN, I remind you - that this man is capable of such a crime".

Simmons left the thought hanging for a moment.

"Now, let's look at three things you need to consider. Means. Motive. Opportunity." He slapped the palm of his left hand with the back of his right three times.

"Let's take opportunity first. We'll get that one out the way. Why? Because my client was in Arnold Cooper's shop that morning. We don't dispute that. Mr Finlay was there, ergo he could have done it".

Thanks a bunch, I thought. Who's side are you on?

"But let's look at means next. My learned friend has contested that Mr Finlay's fingerprints were on the knife used to kill poor Mr Cooper. Yes, they were. But they would be if he'd removed the knife FROM the body, rather than insert it INTO the deceased. And where did this knife come from? The defendant – Mr Finlay – owned no such knife. There is no evidence that he purchased such a knife – and nor, let me remind you, did the knife match the set owned by the victim. You need to ask yourself 'where did that knife come from'?"

Simmons let the question sink in before continuing. "And, let me tell you, 'means' in a legal sense does not just refer to the weapon. It refers to whether the defendant has the wherewithal to commit such a crime. So; I ask you again: does this look like a man who would commit this heinous crime?"

Angus Simmons took a deep breath, sighed audibly. "Members of the jury, we have heard of Mr Finlay's good nature. His sound character. You have been reminded of his clean record, and of the responsible role his employer entrusts him with. No, my friends, James Joseph Finlay does not have the 'means' to commit this crime".

I was listening more intently now. Perhaps there was a glimmer of hope after all. I gauged the faces of the jury. It was impossible to tell, but they didn't look convinced by Simmons' argument. They weren't as attentive as they'd been during Boythorn's performance.

"Finally, we come to motive". Simmons slowed down his speech. Lowered the volume ever so slightly.

"The prosecution would have you believe that this perfectly respectable and respected member of our community took the life of an old man he'd befriended for the sum of £50. You've heard during this trial how the shop was undisturbed. There was no sign of any stock being taken, the till was full, nothing was missing. So my learned friend Mr Boythorn concludes the sole purpose of the murder was to take a single £50 note".

Angus Simmons stopped speaking. Held the silence.

"And this from a man who, only the week before the crime was committed, handled a painting valued at £3,000. Why, I ask you, would Mr Finlay kill for £50 when he had access - 'means and opportunity' – to £3,000?".

The barrister looked pointedly at the prosecution. "Ladies and gentlemen of the jury. My client is innocent. I urge you to find him so".

He turned to the bench. "Thank you, m'lord".

I glanced towards Yeo-Carter expectantly, as if I would know the outcome by the look on his face. I think I probably did.

He struggled to suppress a yawn.

CHAPTER FOUR

Justice Yeo-Carter called for a short recess. Probably to have a strong cup of tea to keep him awake, I thought.

I met with Simmons in a dusty holding cell that smelled of sweat and onions. I lit a cigarette, and asked Simmons how he thought it had gone. He looked grim.

"Hard to tell, James", he said. "Hard to tell".

I asked him again, and he tried to reassure me that he always looked this way after closing speeches. Then he told me he'd done his best and hoped it'd be enough.

The words of a doctor to the relatives of a dying man. Besides, it was written all over his face. I sucked on my cigarette and tried to prepare myself.

"But", he continued, marginally more cheerfully, "we'll know better after Yeo-Carter's summed up. He glanced at his watch. "The old man's probably just had to take a break for his medication".

I didn't know whether it was a lame attempt at a joke, but either way at that point we got the nod to return to the courtroom.

After we'd gone through the 'All Rise' charade one more time, Justice Yeo-Carter shuffled his papers and addressed the jury. I knew it was important to take in what Yeo-Carter was saying. But I just couldn't.

Firstly, he has this awful habit of smacking his lips together at the end of almost every sentence. It grated on me, but not as much as his pronunciation of any word containing the letter 's'. His ill-fitting dentures whistled like a steam train. I found myself anticipating when the Flying Scotsman would make its next appearance.

Besides, Yeo-Carter simply précised what had already been presented during the trial. And he did so by outlining the prosecution stance on each strand of evidence, before saying "On the other hand…" and going on to summarise what my team deduced. Things we'd heard every day for the last three weeks.

After almost an hour of this, he came to the important part: his directions to the jury.

"So", he whistled, "it is your duty to come to a verdict on which you are all agreed. I remind you to judge the matter on the facts and evidence presented during this trial, and on those facts alone. You must decide whether you are satisfied that the prosecution have proved 'beyond all reasonable doubt' – not necessarily conclusively, but beyond reasonable doubt - that James Joseph Finlay murdered Arnold Cooper".

He took a sip of water. Slowly placed a sheet of his notes to one side. Reading from it, he continued.

"I remind you that the prosecution has provided evidence that the accused had the victim's blood on his clothing and handkerchief. His fingerprints were found on the weapon shown to have been used in the murder. The accused had in his possession a £50 note known to have been owned by the late Mr Cooper. And you have heard medical evidence to indicate that the defendant received a blow to the head consistent with being hit with an object which, the prosecution allege, was the walking stick belonging to Mr Cooper, used in a futile attempt to defend himself".

'Phew', I thought. 'Is that all?'

I glanced at Lawrence Boythorn. He sat back in his bench, relaxed and smiling. His hands lay at rest on his portly stomach. In contrast, my brief, Angus Simmons, sat tense and upright, teeth clenched, hands clasped so tightly I could see his knuckles whiten.

Yeo-Carter selected another page of notes. The defence, for their part, have proven that the accused did not own the knife used to kill Mr Cooper".

I waited for him to continue. Waited in vain. My defence, in his eyes, consisted of one solitary shred of evidence. I stared at the floor, both deflated and defeated.

"It is in your hands", Yeo-Carter continued, "and your hands alone, to determine whether the defendant is guilty or innocent as charged, based on these, the facts of the case".

He took another sip of water, scratched the top of his wig. Bizarrely, I thought it made him look like Stan Laurel's father in drag. Yeo-Carter continued his address to the jurors.

"You must now retire to consider your verdict". His gaze fixed on me. "When you have reached a decision on which you all agree, you will return to this courtroom to deliver your verdict."

With that, he stood and shuffled out of his court, shoulders hunched, head jutting forward.

Boythorn beckoned his team towards him and they huddled around him as if in a playground game. The press hurried off to file their copy. The public began to stream from the chamber, their deferential whispering slowly growing in volume as they neared the exit.

Simmons stood alone, gathering his papers together as the jurors filed past me. Most looked steadfastly ahead, refusing to meet my eye. A few looked in my direction. The look they gave was not comforting.

All apart from the middle-aged woman. She alone offered me a sympathetic smile. Perhaps she was my only hope. Perhaps, just perhaps, she would be strong enough. Perhaps the jury wouldn't be able to reach a unanimous verdict.

Perhaps.

CHAPTER FIVE

The cell door slammed shut behind me, the echo a rock falling into my well of despair. The thought of these four walls being my world for the rest of my life was so nearly the ruination of me.

I'd held myself in control for so long that, when the dam burst, the flood came. I threw myself onto the mattress, pulled my knees up to my chest and cried like a baby. Great heaving sobs wracked my entire body until I could no longer breathe. I was a fallen tree, empty and hollow.

I remained that way for twenty minutes or more, all the time aware that twelve people who knew not the slightest thing about me were at that moment deciding my fate.

When I had cried myself dry, I knew I had to pick myself up again. I tried to think positively. I thought of the juror who I could count on; the lady with the smiling face. I thought of Angus Simmons who, despite his relative inexperience, had presented as good a case as I could have wished for. And I thought of Yeo-Carter, thankful that the jury would decide, not him.

I lit another cigarette, drawing more strength from the soothing nicotine as it coursed through me. I even managed to see a positive in the negatives. If found guilty, I thought, at least capital punishment had been abolished. At least I would be alive. Alive to appeal. Yes, the appeal. That would be successful. It had to be.

Slowly, I sat up. Began to be 'me' once more. The cell was cold. I wrapped the blanket around my shoulders. Drew some comfort from the meagre warmth it offered. My breakfast tray sat undisturbed, the wallpaper paste solidifying in the bowl. I craved a fresh cup of tea.

I wiped away my dried tears, rubbed my face until it was ruddy, and shook my head to clear it. I retrieved the newspaper from the tray and settled back on my bunk.

The Daily Sketch unfurled back-to-front, fell open at the football reports. Liverpool's march towards the championship looked unstoppable. Another win; four-nil against Nottingham Forest.

I'd never followed a particular team, going to a game held no appeal to me but, now more than ever, I appreciated the escapism it offered from everyday life. I was particularly enthralled by the drama of the scores slowly unveiling themselves on BBC Grandstand's teleprinter. I often wondered how it must feel to follow a team and experience the anxious wait for the result to be revealed.

I imagined the poor Nottingham Forest fans seeing 'Liverpool 4' appear, then enduring the interminable wait whilst 'Nottingham Forest' slowly scrolled across the screen, hoping against hope for the figure '5' to pop up; all the while knowing that it would show '0'. That brought an ironic smile to my face. It seemed to me to be an allegory of my trial.

I reversed the paper. The front page screamed of Ian Brady and Myra Hindley's court appearance after the discovery of another child's body on Saddleworth Moor. My thoughts were with the parents; all their hopes evaporated by the knock on the door.

My grandmother always believed that life revolved around Hope and Faith; said that Charity would follow like night follows day. Sorry, Gran. It's all nonsense. You can hope all you like. Have as much faith as the Archbishop of Canterbury. Doesn't change a thing. Life's about as charitable as most theatre goers are to the homeless they step over on their way from the opera.

Beyond the front cover, I found a story about the future of Rhodesia. Opposite it, yet another photographic spread taken from atop the Post Office Tower. How longer was the press going to dine out on that one? It's been weeks since Wilson officially opened it, for goodness sake.

I skipped the TV pages. Not much point when I'm locked up for the night by 9. Unless I'm out by then, of course. Fat chance.

I turned another leaf, followed by one more. Then I froze. I lowered the paper. Brought it back up to my eyes. Looked again. It was still there.

Adrenalin coursed through me. I shouted for the guard. I leapt forward. Grabbed the tray. Dragged it back and forth across the bars until it sounded like the rattle of machine guns. I continued to holler until hoarse.

My teleprinter had just revealed '5'.

CHAPTER SIX

"My God".

The voice was that of Alice Timlin. I'd asked for Angus Simmons but the best I could get was a junior member of his team. "Go through that for me one more time, James", she ordered.

The Daily Sketch lay on the table between us. The warder standing behind me craned his neck to see it.

"This story here proves I'm innocent!". I stabbed my finger at the paper so hard I stubbed it on the table beneath. "Don't you see?"

To anyone else, the story was a minor good news story. A filler tucked away next to the horoscopes and above 'Letters to the Editor'. To me, though, it was the best news story in history.

It was a photograph of a lucky punter who had come across a rare stamp; a stamp that had brought him almost £10,000 at auction. The man was pictured smiling into the camera, a wad of notes spread out in his hand like a Geisha's fan.

"Right", I said, drawing in a slow breath. I had to be clear. Didn't have time to be misunderstood. "I've seen this man before. I am – was - always the first customer at Arnold's newsagent's. Except for the day of the murder. Simmons told the court that I'd seen someone leaving the shop that morning before I got there, but the judge had dismissed it. He said it was inadmissible without witnesses. Well, this is him! This is the man who beat me to the shop. I know it is!!"

Alice Timlin shifted in her seat. Laid her pen to rest. "And you say you'd seen him before?".

"Yes! A few days earlier. Arnold had been showing me a photograph of his late wife. Something dropped onto the floor. The man who picked it up – it was him. I'd thought it was a till receipt or an ordinary postage stamp that had dropped out but, don't you see, it was this stamp. The antique one. He must have known its value and come back to get it. At all costs. He killed Arnold!".

Adrenalin coursed through me. The warder put his hands on my shoulder to restrain me. My mouth was dry, my palms sweaty.

Alice looked at me. "Do you think you can prove this, James?"

I slumped back in my seat. "No. Not yet. But it's wrong to say that nothing in the shop had been disturbed. There WAS something missing from it. Arnold's watch, that's what was missing. He kept the stamp inside it, with his wife's photograph. Find the watch. Find it, and my innocence is proven. Find it, Alice. Please – find it for me".

Alice Timlin looked up from her notepad. A smile flickered for a moment, then it was gone. "It's very late, James. The case has been made. The evidence presented. The jury's already out. They may even be coming back as we speak. It may be too late".

Hope began to fade. A shadow crossed my soul. This couldn't be so.

"But I tell you what, James. I'm going to give it a bloody good try. Warder: let me out of here. I've got a barrister to see". Alice Timlin left in a whirlwind of flying papers and twirling skirt. "James – I'll be back. Soon", she called over her shoulder.

"Don't worry. I'm not going anywhere", I shouted after her, but the sound of her heels clicking down the corridor had already faded. The door was triple-locked behind her yet, somehow, the closing of it no longer seemed a portent of doom.

It felt like I'd been looking at life through the wrong end of binoculars for months. Suddenly, everything was sharper, brighter.

Not long after Alice Timlin dashed off to report to Simmons, I'd been transferred to the same musty holding cell I'd been in earlier, except now I could smell lavender and apple blossom, not body odour. I had a smile on my face. I could look to the future with optimism.

I'd been there for less than an hour when the door to the holding cell opened. "Visitors for you", said the policeman on guard duty.

I stood to greet Alice as if I was welcoming her into my front room. She entered, head down. Simmons was with her. He shook his head at me.

"I'm sorry, James". Alice's voice.

I felt the oxygen suck from the room. The air was oppressive, nimbus before the storm breaks. "But you've got the proof. There – in your hand". I pointed to the newspaper she'd brought back with her.

"James, I told you it was late. That it might have been too late. And it was".

"How? What happened?".

It was Simmons turn to speak. "As soon as Alice told me, I went to see Yeo-Carter in his chambers. He refused to see me at first. Said it was most improper. 'What would the Crown say?' he'd asked. I told him there was new evidence, crucial evidence that proved your innocence. He agreed to give me five minutes".

"So you did see him, then. You did speak to him. You – it must have been what YOU said". I was furious. Took my frustrations out on Simmons. "What am I paying you for? My god, you're bloody useless. Do you know that? Useless".

Simmons looked forlorn. It was Alice who came to his defence. "That's not fair, James", she said. "I was there. Angus did his best but Yeo-Cater was having none of it".

"But why? What happened?"

"He did hear me out James" Simmons said. "But he didn't listen to me. He wanted to know if there were any witnesses. If anyone had seen this man leave or enter the shop. Obviously, there isn't any witnesses. No-one had seen hm. Except you. And you're not independent".

"But I saw him. And I told you about his last visit. The stamp, the sweets. The watch, goddamnit. What about the watch?" The binoculars had reversed again. Tunnel vision.

"Angus told him all that, too", Alice said. "He asked if we had the watch. When we said 'no', he asked if there was any proof that it had gone missing. If it had ever existed. When we said we didn't, not yet; he'd dismissed us".

"He can't have. Surely he wants justice, too? That's his vocation; his purpose".

Simmons and Alice looked at one another. "If only it worked that way", Angus said. "He told me that the case had been presented, that none of this had been brought up in evidence, that the jury had retired. It was all inadmissible. He told me that law had a due process which must be followed".

Alice held my hand. "That's when Angus told him the law was an ass".

'Good for you', I thought with new-found respect. 'Well done Simmons'.

"And", said Simmons. "That's when he turned puce and ordered us to leave".

I tilted my head back. Stared at the ceiling. Took in what seemed to be the last vestiges of air within the room; air that was foul once more. "So", I asked. "What happens now?"

It was Simmons who answered. "Now", he said. "We pray. Pray – and start work on your appeal. Just in case prayers don't work".

I managed a laugh.

"Try not to worry, James", Alice said, leaning forward and fixing me with eyes the colour of a Caribbean sky. "I promise I'm going to find that watch. If this jury can't see that your innocent, I can. I'm going to prove it. I'm going to find that watch".

I felt imbued with confidence. What moments ago had seemed a position of no hope had become one of promise.

I was resigned to a guilty verdict. I was resigned to imprisonment. But I knew that Alice and Angus wouldn't let it rest. It may take weeks, it may take months. It might even be a year or two. But I knew I'd be free.

Then the door opened.

"Jury's coming back, son".

CHAPTER SEVEN

So, here we are. Standing in the dock as the jury file in, one-by-one, relief showing on their face that their ordeal is over.

My ordeal may only just be beginning yet I'm feeling strangely serene. No knots in my stomach, no tension headaches, my face doesn't feel pinched or drawn. I know the outcome. I've prepared myself for it. I know where I'm going.

But I also know that Alice and Angus are fighting for me. I know that they'll find the evidence to clear me. And I know that my appeal – when it comes – will be successful. All I need to show is patience. It may take time but, let's face it; I'd soon be doing plenty of that.

Yeo-Carter has taken his place. The clerk of the court is on his feet. "Would the foreman of the jury please rise?".

The foreman stands, self-conscious in his moment of fame. Except it isn't a 'him'. It's a woman. That's unusual in itself. The fact that it's 'my' woman – the smiley woman – makes it more unexpected.

She looks me in the eye, smiles at me again – and nods in my direction. Hope rises within me. Like a boat swelling on the tide, I feel myself lifted. Surely she hasn't persuaded all the others? Not this quickly.

Has she?

I look towards Simmons, expecting him to have read the signs, too. Of course, he hasn't. Neither has Alice. She looks taught. Cold and pale.

I had prepared myself for a lengthy sentence. Thought I was comfortable in the knowledge that Angus and Alice would continue the fight. Perhaps the fight isn't going to be needed.

I battle with my emotions. I don't want to build my hopes up. Don't want my boat to come crashing down on the rocks. So I take a deep breath. Try to position myself back where I was before my ally on the jury got to her feet.

The clerk is speaking again. "Have you reached a verdict upon which you are all agreed?"

"We have".

Unanimous! Well done, Angus. Well done my juror friend! No. Be calm. Not there yet.

"The defendant, James Joseph Finlay, is charged that, on or about the 11th day of July 1965, he murdered Mr Arnold Cooper. Do you find the defendant Guilty or Not Guilty?"

She glances in my direction again. Smiles at me. Again.

I smile back at her. I'm still smiling as she says

"GUILTY".

**

Ok, ok. I'm no worse off than I was five minutes ago. Keep calm. Breathe. Adopt the face that the press describe as 'showing no emotion as the verdict was announced'.

Cocooned in my own little bubble, I hadn't noticed the gallery had become animated, presumably there'd been a few cheers, perhaps a few sympathetic gasps. I'd only noticed there'd been a reaction because the din has subsided and silence returned to the courtroom.

Boythorn stands submerged under his back-slapping team, a Roman emperor in black receiving the acclaim of his senate. Didn't expect anything else from him.

Alice is shedding a tear. That's nice of her.

So, Yeo-Carter: over to you; let's get this sentence out of the way then I can get on with getting out.

"James Joseph Finlay, you have been found guilty of murder; murder defined as the killing of a human being in the Queen's peace, with malice aforethought. It is now my duty as a servant of the Crown to pass sentence on you".

Get on with it.

"You seem to me to be an intelligent man. That makes your crime all the more abhorrent. You befriended a frail and elderly man with the sole intention of taking advantage of him. In short, you took the life of Arnold Cooper in cold blood for the paltry sum of £50"

My grip on the dock rail is so tight my knuckles hurt. This is so unfair; so wrong. I can accept the verdict. I find listening to this dinosaur whistle his way through a litany of defamation much more intolerable. Angus told me to remain calm. God, it's so hard.

"I have listened to the arguments of your attorney, and that of the Crown. I can find no aggravating or mitigating circumstances".

He breaks off to look at me. I'm not giving him the satisfaction of appearing shocked. After all, I know what awaits me.

"I note that you have no prior convictions and are of previous good character. However, I must consider your conduct during this trial. You have shown no remorse or guilt. You refused to take the stand, under oath, to present this court with a defence. The evidence was plain yet you protested your innocence and, thus, subjected these good people of the jury to details most horrific".

A smack of lips followed by a pause for him to take a sip of water. Almost over now.

"We live in evil times. We have heard recently of terrible, terrible events on the Yorkshire / Lancashire border where the lives of innocent children have been taken away by those who have become labelled the Moors Murderers. The law must do all it can to prevent the breakdown of society. Crime and punishment is about protecting the weak and vulnerable. Protecting people like those children, and people like Arnold Cooper".

I notice Alice looking forlorn. I try to catch her eye; to show her that it's going to be all right.

"Mr Finlay, you strike me as being cold, calculating, and unremorseful. The Crown has called on me to impose the maximum possible sentence. I am mindful so to do".

Yeo-Carter makes a strange bobbing motion, as if retrieving something he's dropped. Never noticed that habit in him before. He takes another sip from his glass, lapping it up in every sense.

"The Act under which you are charged is the Homicide Act of 1957. You may deem yourself fortunate that this Act now reserves Capital murder for particularly heinous acts such as murder of a police officer, murder by shooting, or multiple murders. You are guilty of none of these".

Well that's all right, then, isn't it?

"The said Act stipulates that murder outside of these categories – non-capital murder – carries a mandatory life sentence". He pauses for dramatic effect. To let his words sink in.

So, that's it, then. Life. Or 'life' until Angus and Alice find the watch, which they will do, of that I'm certain. Yeo-Carter is still rambling on.

"Mr Finlay, I view all murder as malevolent. What crime can be worse than taking the life of another human being? And that, Mr Finlay, is precisely what you did. You took the life of a helpless innocent in the process of thieving a mere £50".

Out of the corner of my eye, I catch Simmons and Alice look at one another. Boythorn sits up straight.

"So, taking the circumstances of your actions into consideration, and with the Crown's request for severe punishment in mind, I am obliged to pass sentence in accordance with the letter of the law".

Angus and Alice are on their feet.

"James Joseph Finlay, there is one category of Capital murder I did not touch upon earlier. That category is defined in law as 'murder committed in the furtherance of theft'…"

I realise what Yeo-Carter was reaching for a moment ago. I'm shivering, trembling. The courtroom is spinning. I'm going to pass out. I know I am. My vision is beginning to fade, to turn black.

As black as the cap atop Justice Yeo-Carter's wig.

***

EPILOGUE

On that day, Monday the 1st November 1965, two death sentences were passed: one upon a Mr David Chapman, in Leeds Assizes, accused of the murder of a swimming pool attendant; the other on James Joseph Finlay.

Precisely one week later, on the 8th November 1965, the UK parliament passed the Murder (Abolition of Death Penalty) Act. The Act stated that all crimes of murder were now non-capital offences.

As a result of the new Act, the judge in the case of the Crown vs David Chapman reviewed his sentence, ordered a reprieve, and commuted it to life imprisonment. Chapman was released after serving fourteen years. He later died in a car accident.

Justice Mr Maxwell Yeo-Carter, under pressure from Civil Rights Groups and numerous Members of Parliament, also agreed to review the case of James Joseph Finlay.

He found the sentence imposed upon Finlay to be sound and just.

*****

BOOK FOUR

THE REFUGEE

The Refugee

'….But the fountain sprang up and the bird sang down
Redeem the time, redeem the dream
The token of the word unheard, unspoken

Till the wind shake a thousand whispers from the yew

And after this our exile'

Ash Wednesday

TS Eliot

(Faber & Faber)

CHAPTER ONE

The refugee surveyed the alien landscape from an outcrop of barren rock. Nothing stirred out there and, although he had to raise a hand to shield his eyes from the glare of the vermilion skies, he was sure that nothing filled the air above him. But It was the silence that bothered him the most. It enveloped him; wrapped itself around his shoulders like a shroud, closeting him in its vacuum-like stillness.

A wave of melancholy washed over him, tossing his emotions in its ebb and flo as he realised he would never again hear the lark's chorus heralding a new dawn. For him, at least, there was to be only one more dawn, a dawn very different to that which he had been accustomed. A shiver rippled his still-muscular frame, though he wasn't cold.

He scanned the horizon, taking in the desolate terrain; trying to remember how it had once been. He pictured verdant valleys, forests brim-full with life, the sun's rays filtering through swaying branches. His thoughts took him further afield. To distant islands, sun-drenched shores, deep oceans and cloudless skies.

He contrasted his memories with the reality set out before him and wondered how it had come to this. He knew there was nothing for him here now. The emptiness drained him. He'd spent a period of his life homeless, wandering the streets. The feeling of isolation he had experienced then was the only sensation he could compare to the bereft hollowness hanging over him.

He had once been achingly lonely. He sighed at the realisation he was alone again. Except for the Angel, of course. He was still there.

The refugee turned his gaze to a petrified tree stump. Knotted and gnarled, it resembled a varicosed appendage rooted in the orange dust littering the rocky escarpment. Propped against it was the Angel, legs stretched out in front of him, crossed at the ankles. His scuffed golden sandals blended into the rusty dirt. He was leafing through yesterday's grubby newspaper.

According to the Book of Daniel, he seemed to recall from the vestige of a memory somewhere deep inside him, Angels had bodies of topaz, arms and legs that gleamed of burnished bronze. A face like a lightning bolt and eyes that were torches of fire. He who sat before the refugee was the antithesis of what Daniel described. Thin as a reed, pale and wan, wrinkled, rheumy-eyed.

The Angel shifted his weight from buttock to buttock. The movement prompted his once-white vestment to hoist itself at an unseemly angle, displaying way too much milky white thigh. The refugee shook his head. What should have been a wondrous encounter was nothing more than another addition to his long list of shattered illusions.

**

When he'd first stumbled upon the Angel, his initial reaction had been one of apathy. The refugee hadn't been startled or enthralled, nor was he in awe or in fear. It was as if the Angel surrounded himself with an aura that numbed the senses, making his presence seem everyday normal. Or perhaps the brain is wired with some primordial programme to accept and expect such a presence. Either way, the experience didn't move him. He hadn't even flinched when the Angel spoke to him.

"So you found me at last, I see. Don't know why I'm surprised; they always find us in the end. And they always react like you. A blank look on their face. I sometimes wish just one of you would respond a bit differently. Spice things up a bit".

The voice was reedy; a quivering break catching in the throat from time to time. The refugee didn't know what an Angel should sound like, but he didn't think it should be like this.

"Anyway", the Angel had persisted, cutting to the chase. "You need to know a few rules. One: there's a protocol to follow. We all have our place in the hierarchy, and you come below Angels. That means you only speak when I speak to you. Comprendez?"

The refugee saluted and clicked his heels together. The initial mysticism of the Angel must be wearing off. Or he was full of self-bravado. He couldn't decide which.

"Two", the Angel continued, "we mustn't get too close, emotionally like. You don't get to know my name, and I suggest you don't tell me yours. Sounds a good way to start. And, finally,…"

"Don't tell me: Step Three…you kiss and hold me tightly?" The refugee offered. Yep, definitely worn off.

The Angel was not amused. "No. Thirdly, and most importantly, you stay nearby. Don't want you wandering off all by yourself, do we? You might get lost".

The refugee had turned full circle. "Getting lost? There's not a thing in sight. There's no-one else here. How could I 'get lost'?"

"There's always a way. Just don't do it, ok?" Phlegm caught in The Angel's throat and he coughed chestily. He spat the expectorant into the earth.

"Uh-huh". The refugee's positive verbal response was at odds with the negative scowl of distaste on his face. He thought he preferred being under the Angel's spell, or aura, or whatever it had been. He had begun to see the Angel for what he really was. And the downbeat figure had not filled the refugee with confidence or respect.

"Okay", the Angel had said, donning a pair of half-moon spectacles. "I need to make a few notes".

"What?"

"I have to take a few notes. In case they're needed, like".

"Needed for what?"

"All in good time", he'd answered enigmatically. "Just tell me how you came to be here. That'll be a good start".

The refugee had stared off into the distance as he tried to form memories into words. But how do you tell of things forgotten? He'd looked at the hazy burnished glow in the sky, seeking out anything that might give him inspiration. But there was nothing. Nothing to see nor anything to recall.

The Angel saw the struggle in his eyes. "Okay", he said, "I tell you what, if it makes it easier for us to talk, give yourself a name. Remember the rules though, yeah? Make something up".

The refugee thought again for a moment. "I guess you can call me Sam, if you have to".
"Right, Sam. How about you start with your childhood?"

**

And so began their uneasy relationship, neither wholly trusting nor understanding of the other.

There was a moment when the relationship could have become something more tangible. When Sam had explained that he had no specific memories of his early childhood, other than that he was sure it had been joyous, he broke down when he admitted to having no memory of his mother; that it was his father – Pops, he called him - who had brought him up.

Had the Angel reached out to him at that moment, they may have formed a closer bond. But the Angel's rule of 'not getting too close' clearly prevailed. He merely told Sam to take his time, there was no hurry, and had returned to his newspaper leaving Sam to weep alone.

The Angel was in charge whether Sam liked it or not, and it seemed to him that the Angel's silent treatment at his time of need was a deliberate test for him; a kind of mental torture akin to psychological water-boarding.

Despite 'the rules', Sam remembered an old trick of the hostage. Befriend your captor. It was a tactic he'd used before but how do you strike up a casual conversation with an Angel? "Hi. How's God today?" seemed an unlikely opening gambit. Similarly, "Oh I just love your halo – I've been looking for one just like that" didn't sound natural. Besides, he'd come to realise that Angels didn't have haloes. At least not this one.

While Sam pondered on what to say, the Angel proved he was the one in charge; the instigator of all communication. Without looking up from the newspaper, he said "We can continue any time you're ready, you know. You were telling me about your parents".

Sam took a deep breath. He wanted to be the one to choose when to continue his story. Once again, the Angel held the upper hand.

"I guess Pops hadn't had it easy", Sam continued. "Bringing me up alone must have taken its toll but I didn't see it that way. I thought I was 'becoming my own man'. Pops thought I was becoming too big for my boots. The truth probably lay somewhere in-between. He'd been used to doing things his way. He had no need to consider anyone else, no need to compromise. His word stood. As for me, well, I needed space. Let's just say we didn't see eye-to-eye. We argued a lot".

The Angel looked at him reproachfully. *"'Honour thy father and mother'*, remember. One of the Big Ten. I wouldn't go admitting that, if I were you. Carry on, then. Let's see if you can redeem yourself".

Sam paused for a moment, looking around at the desolation surrounding him. What did it matter if his Ps and Qs slipped now? "Well, I didn't like the arguments so I tried covering things up. Not telling him things. The more I hid, the more he became suspicious. I fell in with the wrong crowd. Before I knew it, I was in too deep. Had to cover my tracks and the only way I could do that was to lie".

Sam went on to explain how the inevitable had happened. Spoke about how the time came when a lie over something so trivial that he had no memory of it whatsoever became the final straw for his father. The ensuing row developed into a fist fight, and became the day he chose to leave home. Or rather, the day he was ordered to leave home. It was also the day his life changed irrevocably.

The Angel looked at him over his spectacles and shook his head. "Really? You never learn, do you? That's the second one you've broken in little over half an hour. And I tell you; this one's worse. *'Thou shalt not bear false witness'*. Do you know Proverbs? The Bible, that is, before you come up with a Clever Dick response about 'birds in the hand'"

Sam shrugged his shoulders. "Not as such I don't, no".

"Perhaps you should. *'Seven things are an abomination to Him'*, and all that. In amongst stuff about 'haughty eyes' and 'hearts devising wicked plans', the Lord includes 'a lying tongue' and 'a false witness who breathes out lies'. You're setting your little ducks up in a nice row. That's two of His Abominations down now as well, five to go".

While the Angel spoke, Sam thought about what he had done; how easy it had been to break the commandment. Lies happen so fast, he mused. He thought how beneficial it would be if life had one of those 'Are you sure you want to do this?' prompts. But, even then, he concluded, he'd always clicked 'yes' in life, regardless of the consequences. He consoled himself with the thought he'd have been no better off.

The Angel was talking again. "That's what your conscience is for", he said, reading Sam's thoughts once more. "Life's choices aren't supposed to be easy. Wouldn't be a test if they were. I know it's not for me to say, but you're not coming out of this particularly well at the moment".

"But you're picking out one or two isolated incidents", Sam complained. "Surely that shouldn't decide my fate? Besides, I've spent most of my life doing good. I've only ever wanted to help people. I was a Samaritan for a while, you know. It helped shape the way I lived my life".

"Now we're getting somewhere. Perhaps there might be hope for you yet". The Angel screwed his face up as a sneeze came over him. He caught it between his fingers, glanced at it, then wiped his hand on his tunic. "Hey – I get it now. 'Sam'; short for Samaritan. Nice one. Very clever".

The refugee had lost his train of thought momentarily. He was still disturbed by the sight of an Angel wiping nasal detritus on his vestment. Sam picked up his train of thought again.

"If I have sinned in my life, then haven't we all?", he asked pointedly. "And I've suffered for them. Paid my dues. When I left home I had nowhere to go except on the streets. Believe me, that was hell on earth". He paused for a moment, lost in the horrors that befell him at the hands of others.

He was fortunate that much of that time was spent in a drug and alcohol induced haze. Just occasionally, a faded snapshot of those days filtered into his mind. Sam tried to piece together the grainy images like a jigsaw, order them into a meaningful sequence, but his mind refused to accept them for what they were.

At every flashback his stomach churned and cold beads of perspiration formed on his forehead like morning dew on a meadow. He just knew, somehow, that he had been exposed to deeds so unspeakable that no man should be forced to endure them. Yet they continued to be the spectre that haunted him. And for what? According to the Angel, he had paid no penance.

The Angel interrupted his thoughts. "So let's hear about them, then. These 'good deeds'". He was wheezing like an asthmatic in a hay field. "Your chance to balance the books".

So Sam had started to explain that his experiences had moulded him into the person he was today. How he had vowed no-one should suffer the indignities he experienced. He still bore the scars, both physical and mental, of those days; still suffered the hallucinations arising from the drugs forced upon him by his isolation, his loneliness and his maltreatment.

Sam went on to tell the Angel how his experience as an outcast and the treatment he'd received at the hands of others had driven him to seek asylum elsewhere.

His journey had been fraught, with precious little food or water to sustain him in the cramped environs of his transport. He told the Angel how it had given him time to think, to be thankful for his escape to a land that promised much. It also gave him time to plan what he wanted to do with the rest of his life.

He explained that during the journey he had become obsessed with the thought of devoting himself to the welfare of others. He made a deal with his conscience: he was going to provide a sanctuary for those without a home or a hope.

True to his word, Sam had resolutely turned his life around in his new homeland. It hadn't been easy. In fact, if truth be told, it was damn difficult. He could see in people's eyes that they didn't want them there. They didn't know him yet they didn't like him. How could that be fair and just? He was looked on with suspicion everywhere he went. Yet he was determined to win them over.

Things began to change for him when, for the first time in his life, he managed to get a place of his own. It was humble and sparse but he was proud of it. More importantly, he told the Angel, it had given him a semblance of status within his new community. Ever so slowly, he became accepted, and a door to a new life opened.

He managed to convince a curmudgeon from a local authority to grant him a licence to open up his home as a hostel. Sam spoke about the endless forms he'd had to fill in, the interminable bureaucracy for one so young to go through. The responsibility he'd assumed was onerous. Worse, he'd been naïve and gullible.

He admitted to the Angel that he hadn't properly thought through the implications of allowing strangers into an establishment that was essentially his home. Sam had been too compliant in those early days, bowing to their requests rather than setting the ground rules for his own lodgers. He'd made it too easy for them, he now realised.

Hindsight, eh? It is truly wonderful. But back then, he explained, he had been too enthusiastic. If he was honest, he'd secretly been too glad of the company. He'd have done anything for them.

The Angel had been silent throughout Sam's monologue. Keen to learn whether he'd done enough to convince him, Sam cast a sideways glance towards the figure by the ancient Yew tree.

The notepad lay on the Angel's chest. It rose and fell with every breath. He was fast asleep.

CHAPTER TWO

So that was how it came to pass that the refugee found himself on the edge of the escarpment having wandered away from the sleeping Angel, how he had shielded his eyes from the unnatural blood-coloured heavens, and how he had chosen not to return to the Angel even though he had now roused himself from his slumbers and turned his attention to the newspaper.

Sam felt no urgency to resume a dialogue with an Angel who had clearly expressed disinterest by nodding off whilst he unburdened himself. There would be time for that later. Let's face it, he had all the time in the world.

The barrenness of the earth was an oxymoron to the beauty of the glowing heavens. It brought back memories of the old adage about red sky at night and red skies in the morning. Trouble was, the refugee had no way of knowing whether it was morning or night; whether to be delighted or forewarned.

And that was when Sam first heard it. The sound was little more than a muffled pop, not unlike a sommelier uncorking champagne into his serving towel but, in the lack of any other noise, Sam thought Krakatoa had exploded.

He jumped and looked around, wide-eyed. But there was nothing to see. At least, nothing but the void that was all around him. Sam had the vague notion of a fragrance he should remember, an unpleasant smell associated with his past but it was gone before he could recognise it.

He peered over the edge of the precipice looking for a stone or a rock that may have tumbled down the hillside. Then he heard it again. Behind him this time. A pop followed by something less discernible. A hiss, perhaps, or a ripple of water. It was so brief that he may have imagined it but he suddenly felt vulnerable without the Angel.

He had little respect for him but the companionship had made the seemingly interminable wait more bearable. Now, the arrival of unexpected sounds became an unwelcome interloper in his date with destiny; a destiny that he knew was out of his control. The noise felt threatening to him, somehow.

Sam felt as exposed as a new-born. He needed someone – anyone – at his side. Whether he liked it or not, the Angel was all he had so, despite his misgivings, Sam picked his way over the burnished surface towards the wizened tree stump.

He stirred a few loose pebbles with his toe as he waited to catch the Angel's attention. For some reason, he still felt it right to defer to the Angel. The Angel watched him warily, much as a dog may observe an approaching stranger, but revealed no overt concern or interest. His attention soon returned to the newspaper.

The refugee, frustrated at the Angel's ignorance, felt compelled to break with protocol. "Did you hear that just now? What was it?"

The Angel yawned but did not look up from his newspaper. Nor did he speak.

"I asked if you'd heard that noise. Gave me quite a fright", Sam repeated.

Still the Angel said nothing.

"Oh for God's sake..", Sam cursed, adding quickly with a wry laugh "Sorry – no offence intended".

The Angel looked at him. He showed no sign of appreciating the joke but nor did he seem offended. Instead, he belched loudly and returned his gaze to the newspaper.

"Never mind", the refugee said. "Probably nothing. Forget I spoke".

Typically contrary, the Angel chose that moment to speak. But it wasn't in response to Sam's question. Instead, the words the Angel spoke were so randomly bizarre - so left-field - that, even if the refugee was given his life to live over again, he would never have guessed them.

"Says here on page six there's a woman in Indonesia had two vaginas. She set up home with a pair of identical twins, would you believe". The Angel shook his head. "God truly works in mysterious ways, his wonders to perform".

Sam recoiled, shocked at the crudity of the cherub.

The Angel smiled drolly. "I guess I'm really not living up to your expectations, am I? You think I'm not worthy of my position. But just think: if I'm an Angel, what does that say about mankind?"

Sam didn't want to think about that. He also didn't know where to go with the conversation but, now the Angel was talking, he wanted to keep up the momentum. "Tell me, are there many of your sort among us?"

The Angel looked at him in an odd manner. "'Our sort'?", he questioned, casting yesterday's paper into yesterday's earth.

"You know. Angels".

"You're really not hot on the Bible, are you? About seventy-two thousand of us at our peak. Matthew 26:53. 'Course, our numbers have dwindled a bit since then. Not much call for us now". To emphasise his point, he nodded towards the bleak terrain, forbidding and abandoned as far as the eye could see. "Probably be redundant myself after this".

"So what happens to you next?" The refugee couldn't believe he was having this conversation.

"God knows".

Sam looked at him for any sign of irony. There wasn't a hint of it.
"If you don't know what happens to you, do you know what happens to me?"

"Not my call. When the time's right, I just make sure you get there safely. You'll have a trial, like the rest of 'em. Standards have slipped a bit lately. S'ppose that answers your question about me being an Angel". He roared with laughter. "Anyway, they might let you in; might not".

"They? I thought there was only one God. Who's 'they'"?

The Angel flicked to the back of his notepad, then looked the refugee up and down. "Dunno. Depends. I reckon your probably not Muslim, looking at you. Christian?"

Sam thought it better not to admit to anything so he said nothing.

"Yeah", the Angel continued. "Definitely Christian, I'd say. In that case, according to my list here, it's Gabriel and Michael today. You're lucky Peter's not on call. He can be a right stickler. God doesn't do the judgements Himself, these days. Too many of them. Delegates it out; shares it around, like. Don't really know why. Bit of a charade, really, because just between you and me He already knows whether you'll be suitable for admission".

"But when will I know? HOW will I know?"

"Easy", the Angel revealed. "If you get a white light, you'll know you're in".

"Bloody hell".

"No. That one's a reddish-purple."

CHAPTER THREE

And that was it. The Angel clammed up as quickly as he'd started the conversation. It was almost as if he'd known he'd come very close to crossing a line. However, Sam wasn't going to waste this opportunity. He was going to tell the rest of his tale to the Angel. He wasn't going to leave the Angel with only broken commandments to remember him by.

Sam was determined to let the Angel know that he'd led a good life, certainly by the standards of the company he kept, so he set about telling him how he had devoted himself to befriending those in need.

It hadn't always been easy, he explained. Not all those who needed his care came to him willingly. Often, he went seeking them. He hoped he'd never be accused of coercing them but, sometimes, they did require a little persuasion. That didn't surprise him. He understood why they may be wary of strangers. He knew how he had felt when he first arrived in the country.

The Angel asked him how he had set about making a difference. Sam told him how he'd spent endless hours aimlessly wandering streets looking for those in need. But how, in time, he learnt there were certain places where he could find prospective clients.

He'd first began to find success by targeting pubs. Not the glitzy ones with bright lights and loud music. Experience told him that his clients would be denied access to such establishments, even if they'd wished to frequent them in the first place.

Rather, the refugee would visit those public houses that were 'just around the corner'. The ones in darkened alleys. The ones with paint peeling from their doorframes, more often than not with cracked window panes covered in grime. The ones where you needn't spill someone's pint for them to pick a fight, and the ones where something

– or someone – could always be picked up cheaply, no questions asked.

It was in places like this that those who needed him most could be found.

Recruiting them was not without its hardships. The men were hard, the women arguably harder, and his initial approaches to them often provoked violence. The refugee was an imposing figure, tall and strong, and often had no option but to use his musculature to survive.

Of course, he told the Angel, there were other places where people needed his aid. Sam had once read somewhere that, after family relationship breakdowns, criminal offenders were more likely to end up homeless than any other group in the community. Here, he realised, was an opportunity to make a real difference.

Rather than risk life and limb by approaching random drunkards, he began visiting prisons and jails. Not visiting, exactly. More loitering outside. He had been 'moved on' by officers of the law on so many occasions that he couldn't remember a week when it didn't happen. But that didn't stop him conducting his work.

Whenever the prison doors opened, he was first to greet whoever emerged. He didn't ask what their crime was, didn't care – all he was concerned with was whether they had a home to go to; a family to be with. He was astonished at the numbers needing his help. Within weeks, almost half of those he entertained in the hostel were ex-offenders.

Intrigued and, Sam could tell, impressed, the Angel wanted to hear more. He asked the refugee how he'd reached out to so many over the years. Swelling with pride, the refugee explained that his decision to join the Samaritans had followed. That this had opened up new avenues to him, that he'd discovered those in need of help were often those who had sinned in the past. Karma, he'd thought of it.

He'd broken the Samaritans strict code of conduct by following up leads from his work with them, but he knew he was still helping them. What was wrong with that, he'd asked the Angel, who could merely nod in ascent.

Besides, as word spread of the good he did, he had less need to endanger himself or come to the attention of the law, or abuse his position with the Samaritans. More often than not, prospective clients sought him out. And it meant he was provided with a good living. Charities began taking note of his hostelry. Many sad cases were referred to him and his home was almost always full to capacity, frequently oversubscribed.

The Angel looked less than happy when Sam had started talking about money. "So you were in it for the money", he had concluded.

"No. Not at all. Exactly the opposite, actually. Money was the last thing on my mind when I opened the hostel. All the bursaries I received – and, yes, there were plenty – went towards extending the premises. I'd say the funds were ploughed back into the business but I don't want you thinking that I viewed it as a business. All I wanted was to provide shelter for more. I welcomed all-comers, no matter what their background was. I never asked questions. And you know why? Because questions demand answers and one of the rules of my house was that there must be no demands".

The Angel was scribbling away furiously, keen not to miss anything. Sam told him that he had made a good host because he knew what loneliness was like. His door was always open and no expense was spared in order to teach his guests that their life could be made worthwhile, the way he had succeeded in turning his life around.

He explained that he'd fed and clothed his tenants, something that was way beyond the call of duty. He gave them shelter and warmth from the cruel world outside, sharing with them an empathy for the horrors they had gone through.

Sam paused for a moment, allowing himself a rare moment of introspection. "I sacrificed the best years of my life for them. I'd no time to venture far from home; to seek a wife or see much of the world. But that didn't concern me. After everything I'd faced in my life, I was content with their company in the knowledge of the good I did for them. I hope it doesn't sound arrogant, but I became their world and they mine. Through no fault of their own, they had nowhere else to go. Society had rejected them just as it had once rejected me. They had no-one and, before I opened the hostel up to them, I had no-one. It had been the perfect arrangement. In the beginning".

Sam seemed pleased at the Biblical reference but, when he looked at the Angel, the refugee noted he had stopped writing. He looked tired, grey-faced and old. But Sam was relieved to have had the opportunity to put forward his case. He was content in the memory of those early days; of the pleasure he gave to others simply by being a friend when they had no other. And of the pleasure he obtained from their company.

Little was he to imagine the difficulties that were to come, and how his hospitality was to turn against him. Although he tried to put the thought behind him, sometimes he felt that his guests rarely deserved such kindness. Seldom did they thank him. Indeed, in his low moments, he sometimes wondered if they'd prefer to face life – or even death – without his aid, such was their lack of gratitude. There were times that he had to prevent himself from revealing bitterness towards them, hoping that, deep down, his guests recognised him as a good man.

Certainly better than the unshaven, crude and sullen figure by the tree. He watched with disdain as the Angel drifted once more into a snoring slumber.

**

Laden with frustration, the refugee thought it better to leave the Angel to his sleep. He didn't want to risk saying or doing something that may jeopardise his future, not when he'd just started to balance the books. He had no reason to believe that recent events took any precedence over historic acts but he wasn't going to leave anything to chance.

By now, Sam had grown accustomed to the peculiar ochre light. It was still uncomfortable, of course, but he could bear a little discomfort. He'd had sufficient practice lately. The Angel had warned him not to leave his side but nothing could be imminent, he concluded, if the Angel felt able to snooze. He decided to explore more of his surroundings.

He found it difficult to walk; like wading through treacle. He couldn't decide whether it was a result of the vacuum-like atmosphere, the thick carpet of cloying ankle-deep dust, or simply age catching up with him. But, whichever, it would have been easier to run in a dream. He was breathing heavily within a few strides.

He picked his way over the rubble-strewn surface with great care. A gelatinous coagulant broiled to the surface from a fissure in the earth's crust. He paused to inspect the mass for a moment before gingerly stepping over it. The smell of sulphur rent the air.

A boulder he stepped on rocked slightly, causing him to stumble. The refugee fought to keep his balance and what should have been a simple task proved to be an exertion in this atmosphere. A sweat broke to his brow though the temperature felt strangely neutral.

In time, he reached the far side of the promontory. He stood on the edge of the escarpment, staring out over nothingness. There was little to see other than a landscape devoid of colour, life, movement and noise. Once again, it was the utter silence that bugged him the most.

The view, such as it was, seemed to shimmer and shift, as if observed through a thin film of water. Here and there, he managed to pick out an object that may have been the remnants of something once recognisable. Far below him, the charred embers of a shapeless entity emitted a faint glow. How apt if it were a bush, he thought, although the lack of any vegetation made it impossible.

He raised his eyes skywards. The heavens remained burnished ochre without the presence of a sun, but cloud-like shapes gathered in the distance. Time to return.

As he turned to set out, he was alarmed to see his path littered with sulphuric geysers. Even as he watched, he heard the familiar pop he recognised from earlier before a serpentine hiss escaped from a fissure to his right; a foul smelling bubble of thick reddish-brown matter emerged from it. Then another formed to his left. And one to the left of that.

The face of the escarpment erupted in boils.

He picked a path between them, each eruption requiring him to change direction, to lose time. He had turned back on himself now, the route to the Angel blocked by the pus oozing from the earth's core. The stench of rotten eggs filled the air.

The light began to fade at the same moment as he realised he'd lost his bearings, so often had he veered from his original course. Much as the ocean adopts shades of blue and sapphire from the sky, then the earth beneath the refugee's feet reflected the darkening of the skies.

Gone were the vivid oranges and crimson to be replaced by the leaden grey of the heavens. It wasn't that the sun had set, for there was no sun. The sky had simply changed colour.

Clouds advanced across the horizon like an army; an army with swollen bellies heavily pregnant with a brewing storm. Something within him told him he must reach the Angel before the storm broke. Was he still heading towards the Angel? He had no way of knowing.

He sensed, rather than saw, the shape of a massive boulder looming in front of him. It was the size of a double-decker bus and he knew he would have a clearer vantage point from its top. He searched for a path towards it that was free from detritus.

He finally spotted a clear opening to it. Estimated it to be about eighty paces from him. He lengthened his stride despite the fact that his legs felt shackled as in a chain gang. His lungs burnt with the effort.

In the gathering gloom, he stumbled over something in his path. Whatever it was, it felt like talons clawing at his legs. He felt his skin tear as he pulled away from it, only for his foot to land in a pool of evil-smelling gelatinous goo.

It sucked at his foot, the brownish matter clinging to him. He struggled to lift his foot from the surface. He managed to raise it a few inches but the rank glue still hung from it like a melting icicle.

He panicked, flapped at it with his arms much like a schoolgirl who'd run into a cobweb. Sam tried to pull the substance off with his hands. There was a sickening smell of burning flesh as the effluent clung to his fingers, hot as hell. He screamed. Almost blacked out with the pain. An explosion of stars lit up his vision until the agony began to recede.

He held his sleeve in his mouth and pulled until a sliver ripped off. He bound it around his damaged hand as best he could to prevent the flesh peeling before knotting it in place with his teeth. He had to keep going. Nothing would halt the impending storm so he couldn't allow anything to slow him.

At the foot of the boulder he searched for anything that might give him purchase. A small crevice just above head height was all he could find. As he stretched for it with his good hand, he heard a thousand voices whispering in his ears. Or was it the sound of the wind that had struck up to support the onward rush of forbidding clouds? He couldn't be sure. Couldn't afford the time to wait; no time to determine what was real and what was imagined.

His hand lodged in the cleft. He grimaced, certain that something other-worldly lurked within. When nothing grabbed him, he flexed his arm and muscled himself a few inches off the ground. The refugee's feet scrabbled across the upward slope of the boulder until they found a ledge to rest upon. He paused for breath, taking in great gulps of air mixed with sulphur. He retched before searching for another handhold. He repeated the motion. And again. And one final time.

Finally, agonisingly, the climb was over. The feeling of euphoria when he first sat atop the rock was like nothing he'd experienced. Although everything around him remained battleship grey, Sam gained a more three-dimensional view of his surroundings from his elevated position. He could see the Angel. So near yet so far away.

Sam was able to map a course to the Angel across the minefield of noxious geysers. His initial plan was to take as direct a route as possible. It would require him to slalom his way around the fractured crust and toxic pools, and there was no guarantee his route wouldn't be cut off by fresh eruptions. His mind was made up for him when several tears ruptured the earth's surface in front of his eyes. He needed an alternative.

He noticed that the fissures avoided the precipitous edge of the overhang. If he skirted the ridge to his right, he realised, he had an unobstructed path. It would take him perilously close to a sheer drop onto jagged rocks below. It would also take him longer. Looking skywards, he saw that the portentous storm clouds had made headway, but not as much as he had feared. There was still time.

Elated that he'd spotted an opportunity, he prepared to shin down the boulder. He paid little heed when he heard the hiss of gas escaping from another crack nearby. The hiss deepened in tone. Increased in volume. Became a rumble. Didn't stop. The boulder shook. The earth's surface rippled until it resembled sand left by a departing riptide as the crack opened up.

It kept widening, became a chasm, poisonous brown ejaculate pumped from it like a fountain. Directly in front of the rock on which he stood.

The stench was overpowering. Rotten eggs, rotten vegetation, rotting flesh. It was if the earth had opened its bowels. The refugee couldn't remember when he'd last eaten but the contents of the meal emptied at his feet along with his bile and digestive juices.

Wiping vomit from his chin with his good hand, he shook his head to clear his vision. His heart sank. In front of the boulder was a cavernous split in the earth's crust, filled with a thick soup of bubbling matter.

The refugee looked across towards the Angel, overwhelmed by a feeling of hopelessness. They were separated by his personal Styx.

With no boatman to help him across it.

CHAPTER FOUR

A wave of desperation swept over Sam. His thought process was drowning in a sea of futility. He knew he didn't have time for self-pity but what else was there for him?

Then, like a piece of flotsam from the wreckage, a thought surfaced. Something he seemed to remember from his climb. He needed to check it for himself. And he had no time to lose.

He launched himself down the rock, his hands and feet barely making contact with the surface. The ground raced up to meet him but still too slowly for his liking. Throwing himself prostrate, he looked at the base of the rock. He was right. The boulder wasn't lying flat on the surface. Instead, it was balanced on a pointed edge set in the barren ground. And it was on a downward slope. If he could only pivot it slightly, its momentum may take it downhill. If it did, it might even wedge itself in the chasm.

'I don't have a boat', he thought. 'But I might have a bridge'.

Renewed with hope, he braced himself against the boulder and began to push with all his might. In a matter of seconds, he'd stopped pushing. He was in agony. The flesh of his burnt hand was raw, weeping from even such brief contact with the abrasive surface.

Breathing deeply until the pain subsided, taking in a lungful of sulphurous air as he did so, the refugee leant into the rock with his shoulder and heaved. He pushed at it, thrust himself at it, ran at it and shouted at it until he could take no more. It didn't move an inch.

He turned his back on it and leant against it. And pushed again. Nothing.

He lay on his back in the dusty ash, put both feet against the rock, and pushed even harder. It didn't budge.

He stood and put his shoulder to it for the second time. He took a deep breath, held it, and heaved once more. Every muscle and sinew ached with the build-up of lactic acid. His face turned puce with the effort. His eyes bulged. Capillaries within them burst turning his vision red.

And then he felt the boulder move. Just an inch, but it had moved.

He sank to the ground, exhausted yet exhilarated. He took in huge gasps of air as he prepared to push again. Worse thing he could have done. The poisonous fumes raged through his system, building on those he'd already inhaled.

His vision swam. He leant back, head resting against the rock, and coughed violently. Couldn't stop coughing. Coughing and retching. He spat on the earth. His spittle was deep red.

He wondered if this was the colour the Angel had warned him about. It was the last thought he had before he lost consciousness.

**

Sam opened his eyes. He lay in the charcoal ash and faced the grey sky. Something felt different. He was strangely lethargic, unable to make sudden movements. Nothing was quite in focus.

He lay gathering his thoughts; his breathing shallow. Staring up at the sky, he noticed it shift. A patch of greyness dissipated to be replaced by a circle of rich golden amber; much like the colour the sky had once been.

The contrast was stark. It hurt his eyes to look into the vivid brightness again after so much monochrome. As he watched, another patch appeared close by it. Windows in the sky. Portals, even. The refugee thought they looked like eyes gazing down on him.

And then, very slowly, very deliberately, the eyes blinked.

Had he been mistaken? He watched intently. Yes, he had imagined it. Just as his pulse rate began to subside, the eyes in the sky blinked again. No mistaking it this time.

The refugee tried to jump to his feet but he couldn't move. His brain told him to go, but his body wouldn't respond. The colours in the portal eyes began to swirl, a mix of crimson and orange hues. Faster and faster like a heavenly maelstrom.

Sam grew dizzy. He closed his eyes only for the kaleidoscope to continue, now in black and white; positive and negative, until it went so fast the shades became a blur, merging into one shade of grey. The grey of the earth, the sky, and the menacing storm clouds building within it.

He opened his eyes to see those storm clouds directly overhead. Only they appeared to be more than clouds. They'd taken on a presence. They were huge, grotesque beings.

One seemed to leer down at him. The cloud-being developed a protuberance: a gross, engorged phallus. It raced onwards, closing in on a second cloud monster. A gap opened in the other raincloud, exposing lurid reds and pinks within it. They rammed together, mounting like rapacious honeymooners.

The spawn of their union - a bolt of lightning – flicked earthwards like a serpent's tongue. It scorched the surface where it alighted, setting ablaze the bone-dry surface.

Thick black smoke rent the air. The refugee's nostrils filled with the smell of decay, so omnipresent that he could taste it. He gagged and retched though there was nothing left within him to spew.

Then the whispering sound began again. Sam strained to hear. It came from the centre of the smoke. Through its wispy tendrils, the outline of figures emerged. Black, faceless, androgynous spectres.

They didn't move. They simply stood before him, waiting. 'What are they waiting for?', Sam wondered.

Another sound emerged above the whispering. Faint and indistinct at first, a vague pounding like distant tribal drummers beating out an eerie tempo. The staccato rhythm gained momentum. Began to sound less like drums. More like the clickety-clack of sticks clashing together.

As the volume increased, so the pace of the beating grew faster; so fast that the clattering resembled a windmill in a hurricane. The crescendo built ever closer. Close enough for him to realise what the sound was. Close enough to realise it wasn't sticks.

It was bones. Bone on bone.

The rattle of bones.

The cloud of black smoke began to pulsate, alive with something evil within. It bulged and flared, the cacophonous noise building inside. Then the smokescreen ruptured.

From out of its depths rose a flock of featherless, skeletal birds. Dozens of them, circling upwards for a moment, turning the air black with their shadowy forms.

The spectral figures watched the carrion pore from the depths of the earth and raised their heads to follow the flight of the flock. Then the spectres stretched out their arms towards the refugee.

The devil birds spotted them. Turned their gaze towards the object of the pointing. Turned their gaze towards Sam. The flock screeched in unison. Turned as one. Swooped towards him.

The clickety-clack of their bony wings filled his ears. Sam sensed the rush of air as the delta flocked downwards, felt their wings batter his frame as they alighted upon him. Talons tore at him, ripping his garments, cleaving through Sam's flesh like their raptor forefathers.

The look on his face was one of surprised fascination rather than horror as he looked down to see layers of yellow fat oozing from the gaping wound where his stomach had once been. Thick clots of blood coated his lower abdomen, ran down his thighs and coagulated on his legs.

Then it became visceral.

Still more of the creatures descended, fighting each other to reach his innards. Sam saw his intestines unravel as first one bone bird then another heaved them out of his body cavity as if they were pulling earthworms from moist soil.

Two of the larger carrions left the meat to the smaller creatures. They landed atop Sam's head, their claws cruelly hooking around his ears. Instinctively, he raised his hands to cover his eyes. But they weren't interested in his eyes. They were after something much more precious to them.

In perfect synchronisation, they jutted their heads back before thrusting their massive bills forward with the force of jackhammers. His skull was cleaved open as easily as an egg, the bone-birds fighting amongst themselves for the grey yolk as it seeped from the gaping cranium.

The refugee's arms spasmed upwards, revealing his face to the hungry flock. As the first of the razor-sharp beaks found the gelatinous gristle of his eyes, he had time for only one thing: to emit the howl of the dying.

His agonising falsetto scream echoed through the silence to eternity.

CHAPTER FIVE

He screamed. His eyes shot open. Bathed in sweat, his chest rose and fell like waves in a storm. Sam lay flat on his back, the lifeless sky above him.

The sky…it was lifeless. No skeleton birds. And he could see it. He could see the sky! The refugee put a hand to his face. Poked his finger in his eye. Ouch – it hurt. It hurt because his eye was still there.

He sat bolt upright, looking around. There was no smoke, no ghost figures. Had he dreamt it? The air was rank with a sulphurous odour. Sulphur and something rotten.

That was it. He'd been overcome by the poisonous effluent that had curdled in the rotting belly of the earth, its toxins infecting mind and body. A hallucination brought on by noxious fumes. Of course – he should have recognised it; he'd had many a bad trip in the past. Relief flooded over him. He sighed and sank his head back until it rested on the ground.

Something about that simple act troubled him, nagged at him like a toothache.

It hit him like a slap in the face. His head was on the ground. It should have been resting up against the boulder.

He was on his feet in an instant. The boulder was gone, leaving gashes and gouges on the surface where it had once been. He hardly dared look around. When he did, he saw the boulder lodged snugly in the huge fracture in the earth's crust. Tears of joy ran down his cheeks. He had a pathway to the Angel.

A rumble of thunder brought him back to earth. The storm was nearly upon him. No time to lose, no time for Plan B. He sprinted towards the boulder, no longer fettered and chained by the heavy atmosphere. He bounded over the rock-bridge, arms outstretched to aid his balance, and leapt onto the dirt at the other side, rolling on his shoulders before settling on his knees.

Sam sprang to his feet. Set off again, striding over fissures and geysers, leaping from side-to-side as if to avoid a sniper's line of fire.

Neck and neck, the refugee and the cloud army raced to be first to the Angel. Ghost-like shadows danced across the landscape. Every step he took became haunted by them. But he was going to win; he was going to reach the Angel in time.

Until the earth opened up beneath him once more and trapped his foot in its maw.

Caught like a bear in a trap, the refugee closed his eyes and, for the first time since childhood, he began to pray.

**

The grip on him was vice-like. Then he realised the grip was not on the ankle around which the evil smelling gunge sucked and bubbled. It was under his armpit.

He opened his eyes. The Angel stood above him, one hand resting on the refugee's shoulder, the other supporting it from beneath. It was the same Angel, of that he was sure, but the eyes burnt brighter, piercing and bejewelled. With what appeared to be minimal effort, the frail Angel raised the refugee's bulk from the crack in the earth's crust. The cloying mud-like substance sucked at the leg one last time then withdrew into the fissure, defeated, leaving only limpet-like patches clinging to his singed clothing.

Sam was free. He looked at the Angel with renewed respect.

"Thank you. Dear God, thank you. You just saved my life".

"Bit late for that, sunshine. Though I might have managed to save your afterlife if your luck's in".

"God preserve me. I've seen Hell".

"Hell, no. Purgatory, perhaps". He looked the refugee up and down. "Mind, I still wouldn't put your odds at getting through it any better than 50:50. What do you think you were doing, anyway? There was a reason I told you not to stray from my side", the Angel lectured.

"I know. I'm sorry. But you were nearby. I guessed you wouldn't let me come to any harm. I thought I'd be safe with my guardian Angel watching over me".

"'Guardian Angel'? I'm AN Angel, yes. Not your guardian Angel, lad. There's no such thing. Do you think we're in some sort of fairy tale?"

"I don't know what we're in. I don't know where we are, or what anything is any more. All I do know is that I want to leave this place. Can we go, please? Now".

The Angel seemed to wither in stature; to return to his previous incarnation. The Angel rubbed his bloodshot eyes and looked at the leaden sky. Colossal hammer-head storm clouds towered above them, apocalyptic harbingers gathering in congress.

"Be patient. It's almost your time", he whispered in hushed reverential tones.

Events moved with a rapidity that left the refugee gasping. A soundless wind lashed at his face with the ferocity of a cat o' nine tails. It grabbed at his hair, had the effect of G-force on his cheek muscles. Yet the wind stirred nothing else.

The brooding clouds raced onwards and downwards until they enveloped him completely, dark snow falling from their menacing guts.
The refugee couldn't remember being as afraid as this. Not gut-wrenching, panic afraid. Even during his worst moments in life, in whatever land; even during the last few hours, he'd never felt like he did now. Unless such memories were banished to dark recesses left

undisturbed for so many years, the moment the sky rolled in on itself and collapsed towards him like a punctured balloon was the singular most frightening event imaginable.

A crack of thunder louder than anything he had ever heard before ripped the sky asunder. A sleeve of iridescent light reached down for him and cocooned him in its radiant blue / whiteness, illuminating the remnants of the shattered earth.

Transfixed in terror, the refugee's senses reeled until they finally absorbed the scrambled message.

White. It was white. Not red.

He swung a glance at the Angel with the swift nervousness of a stalked sparrow. The Angel shook out his crumpled wings and, with a laconic nod of his head, confirmed that this was the moment for which the refugee had both yearned and dreaded. The day he was to be reacquainted with his maker.

Euphoria and despair swept over him. He knew he was about to encounter the beginning of the end, and the end of the beginning.

**

Sam took one last look at the crumbling, deserted world beyond the arc of neon. He was pleased to be leaving it behind, he decided. He may have been unable to remember much about the first tenants to arrive at his hostel but in these, his final moments, he had no difficulty recalling the last.

One was the cherubic faced neo-Oriental man in the starched, buttoned-up tunic and oddly shaped black cap. The blame for all his present troubles could be laid directly upon this one's broad shoulders. Even with his benevolent nature, Sam had found it hard to warm to him. As it was, after his arrival the refugee's hostel had been flooded by droves of visitors desperately seeking shelter and solace.

Sam was reluctant to admit it, indeed he probably never would, but they included characters so loathsome and evil that even his benevolence could not bring himself to admit them. But he was powerless to bar them – he was heavily, overwhelmingly outnumbered and before long his hostel - his home – was theirs. Not for the first time in his life, the refugee was an outcast from his own abode.

And it was all due to the chubby Oriental's distaste for his neighbour and his liking for vermillion sunsets. If only he had refrained from breaking open his billion-dollar toy, life – and death – would have continued as normal.

As the shaft of light drew Sam slowly skywards like a Phoenix from the earth's ashes, the Angel fluttered alongside the luminescent tunnel as unsteadily as a drunken sailor.

The Angel had begun to smile. For a moment, Sam didn't know why. Then he looked at his hand and understood.

The burns inflicted by the malevolent goo began to heal in front of his eyes, the flesh smooth and unblemished beneath. Sam's face displayed wonderment and bemusement at the same time, causing the Angel's smile to broaden.

Sam felt warm. Contented. At ease with himself for the first time in eons. The light around him grew in intensity. His clothes fell from him, leaving him naked as God intended.

The refugee saw the Angel's face change at the sight of his exposed frame. Saw him mouth the word 'No'. Watched as the Angel pounded his fists against the illuminated funnel. Looked on as he desperately sought an entry point with his hands, a mime artist confronted by his glass wall.

And the refugee laughed at the irony of it all. The laugh was deep and resonant.

It stemmed from the very tip of his forked tail.

Satan himself - too virtuous for Hell.

BOOK FIVE

A FALL BEFORE PRIDE

CHAPTER ONE

The sheet stained red. Still it flowed, a ragged spidery-trail spreading across and downwards. Finally, mercifully, it stopped; life-force spent. The witness to the carnage smiled.

"Finished, Mum", Anna squealed. She snapped the red cap back atop her pen, ripped the sheet from her notepad and strode heavy-footed towards the kitchen door.

Ellie Darnell turned from the bubble-strewn sink. She held her hands, encased in yellow gloves, out in front of her like a surgeon scrubbed for surgery. Somehow, she managed to maintain an air of dignity despite her plastic apron in the design of a bestockinged French maid.

"Already?" she smiled, noting with dismay the ketchup stain on Anna's freshly laundered cardigan. "That took no time at all, did it darling? Let's see, then".

Dexter Monroe, orange-tanned teen idol, superstar and all-round good egg was the object of Anna's desires and the subject of her written efforts. His personal fanzine – 'Dextyle' – had offered a chaperoned 'Date with Dex' to whichever of his adolescent fans penned the most adoring fan letter.

Only problem was, Anna wasn't adolescent. She was twenty-nine.

Holding the page gingerly between thumb and index-finger so as not to smudge the proudly-presented item ('it may be good for hands but lemon-liquid won't do anything for Dex's fake-tan', thought Ellie),

Mrs Darnell paid the briefest of attention to the page as she scanned it.

"Very good, darling", she said a little too quickly to be genuine. "But remember thousands love Dex as much as you. You won't be too disappointed if you don't win, will you?" She hoped she'd brought her gently back to earth. Inwardly, she cringed at what she had just read, ashamed at being ashamed.

"Has Nina seen it yet?" Ellie asked, hoping to transfer the burden of guilt to her youngest daughter.

"No, she's reading", replied Anna. Her bright yellow Spongebob slippers scuffed at the floor. "I know what I'll do – I'll read it to Dexter. He'll tell me whether he likes it or not!"

Anna turned on her heel and thumped up to the stairs to her Monroe-memorabilia filed room where she read her efforts aloud to the chocolate-brown eyes melting down at her from the bedroom wall.

**

In time, Mrs Darnell finished her chores and retired to the lounge. Anna had returned from her room and sat alongside her sister. Ellie relaxed opposite them, her eyes on her girls rather than the TV. The phrase chalk and cheese could have been made for them.

Nina, tall and willowy, sat cross-legged and barefoot on the sofa, her golden mane of tousled curls hanging loosely around her shoulders. She grasped a cup of coffee between her thighs with way more confidence than befitted her years.

The ebullience of the 'One Show' presenters gave way to Dot Cotton's monotone as Ellie's gaze drifted to her eldest daughter. She compared Nina's lightly perfumed hair with the lank dark locks that framed Anna's rotund and plain face.

Ellie's eyes misted over as she recalled the time it was confirmed – how had the doctor put it? that Anna was "unlikely to fulfil the potential of a normal person", cruelly but intentionally emphasising the word 'normal'. A lump rose in her throat as she remembered her first reaction had been 'whatever will the bridge club think?'

She reproached herself for it, but often wished Anna had been confined to a wheelchair, or used a white stick. At least that way, people would acknowledge her disability; would empathise and sympathise. But because Anna was outwardly normal, no-one wanted to know.

Ellie's husband had passed away eight years ago. A heart attack. She was convinced it was precipitated by the strain of caring for Anna. Since the day he died, she'd had no-one to share the burden. And, yes - it was a burden. Ellie couldn't pretend otherwise.

Nina was too young. Ellie's relationship with her middle daughter, Karen, had always been fractious. Their bond had all but broken entirely when Karen had walked out after another family row, setting up home with an unemployable musician of dubious stock. Ellie had no desire to be introduced to him, and never had.

The rhythmic beats of an Eric Prydz production jarred Elie from her self-pity. She clasped a hand to her chest in shock whilst Nina reached under a cushion for her mobile phone.

"For heaven's sake, Nina", gasped Ellie. "What a fright. Whatever happened to normal ringtones?"

Nina managed to smile back as she glided through the living room to the hall. She flipped open the phone cover and spoke into the mouthpiece.

After the briefest of pleasantries, Nina glanced over her shoulder and said "The rhubarb is growing cold tonight", in the contrived style of an agent in an old Harry Palmer movie, giggling as she did so.

Her mother frowned at her youngest but turned away when the giggles turned to belly-laughs as the unheard – and probably unrepeatable – response came.

Ellie had become used to Nina's cryptic calls, usually from a boyfriend several years older and without a clue to her age, but Mrs Darnell's face betrayed the unease she felt about such things.

By the time Nina returned, the TV had been switched off. A heavy silence haunted the room. Ellie shivered and headed upstairs, intent on running a bath. As she opened the taps, she remembered with fondness the days she could actually talk to her daughters. Now, barely a word passed between them.

She pursed her lips as she thought of her regret at the way she had let her own friends drift away during the years she devoted to Anna. Nina had plenty of friends, all right, and Ellie always made them welcome. But, no matter how busy her home was, she felt a stranger amidst the teen and twenty-somethings who filled her house.

As Ellie Darnell lay back in the steamy water of her bath, the sounds of a retro radio channel filtered upstairs.

"Loneliness", sang a strangulated falsetto, "Is a crowded room".

Ellie Darnell could have refilled her bath with her tears.

CHAPTER TWO

Nina was leafing through The Independent when the doorbell chimed. She was at the door almost before Ellie heard it ring.

Nina swung open the frosted glass door. Both girls looked at one another for a moment then, almost together, said "Hi, sis" before exchanging high-fives and fist bumps.

The bubble from Karen's gum smacked back into her lips. Nina stepped to one side and allowed her sister to breeze past her into the hallway. Karen raised a quizzical eyebrow. "In the bath", the younger girl whispered.

Upstairs, Ellie quickly towelled herself dry and slipped on a Kimono-style robe that had been her husband's last gift to her. A visit from Karen filled Ellie with trepidation. They were as rare as an honest politician and usually meant one thing – trouble.

Ellie wiped away a patch of steam in the bathroom mirror. Just enough for her to check that the smile fixed on her face didn't appear too insincere.

She glided downstairs like a ghost and barely had time to catch a glimpse of her rebel daughter's latest look before her spectacles misted over – probably caused by leaving behind the humid climes of the bathroom, but almost as likely to have been due to the frostiness of the curtly-nodded welcome she received from Karen.

She removed her glasses to get a better look at Karen's reaction as Anna pushed her written drivel into Karen's hand.

"Hi, Anna. What's this?"

"It's my letter to Dex. I'm going out with him, you know. At least I will be when he sees this. What do you think of that? Aren't I lucky?

No - isn't HE lucky?"

"If you say so, Anna. Not my type, I'm afraid. You know me – I prefer my lovers like my coffee. Black and strong."

Ellie bit her lip. 'Don't bite back', she reminded herself.

"Speaking of which", Karen continued, "Get the kettle on, Nina. I'm drier than a nun's.."

"Karen!"

Karen rolled her eyes at her mother and held her hands up. "Ok, ok. Black and strong, Nina, please", she said with a wink.

Ellie shepherded Anna back into the living room, unprepared to subject her to any more crudity. Karen stayed in the kitchen chatting with her younger sister whilst she prepared the coffee.

Once back in the living room, Karen flopped onto the sofa next to Nina. They continued their conversation. Although Karen regularly raised the mug of coffee in her right hand to her lips, the slip of paper in the left remained unmoved.

Ellie Darnell felt her hackles rise and could contain herself no longer. "Will you two stop your chatter for just one minute and read Anna's letter? You've barely acknowledged her presence, Karen my girl."

"Sod off, mother", she said with a lack of malice. "I'll read it soon enough. But Nina's here, too. I can't ignore her".

"Why not? You've done a pretty good job of ignoring me these last four years, and…"

"Karen's right, mum", interjected Anna. "There are three of us, you know".

Ellie cast her eyes downwards. 'Et tu, Brute?", she thought. Where once she had stood tall and no-nonsense, now she felt stooped and conquered.

Her outburst had the desired effect, though, for Karen's gaze had drifted to the page in her hand. Anna stared into her sister's eyes looking for clues to her reaction, hoping for a seal of approval.

Ellie, too, watched Karen read. Although her daughter's face wasn't classically beautiful, she was blessed with stunning lips for which a botox-addict would kill. They rescued her face from anonymity and, coupled with regular changes of image, presented a striking appearance. Ellie marvelled how Karen could transform herself into the stunning figure before her.

Her natural mousey hair, dyed coal black, was cropped military short. She had an exaggeratedly long fringe which, although slicked back, repeatedly flopped over her left eye causing her to sweep her hand through her hair and toss back her head in a manner that irritated Ellie. She had no doubt that men would be thoroughly enticed by the gesture.

Those God-given lips were a crimson slash on an otherwise chalk-white canvas. A single cross hung from Karen's left ear, glinting in the light from the ornate table-lamp behind her like the golden hues of Autumn caught in evening sunlight.

Ellie dragged her eyes away. She'd become uncomfortable in the silence she'd created. "How's Danny?", she felt obliged to ask.

"Oh, you know Danny, mum", Karen countered, sweeping back her hair for the umpteenth time. "Horny as Hell".

All three girls laughed, Anna more in a Pavlovian reaction to her sister's merriment than anything else, and only Anna cut short her laughter at her mother's tut of distaste.

Ellie wondered what Eric would have made of all this. Her eyes rested upon the gilt-framed photograph of her late husband with the three girls. Three more dissimilar sisters one could never imagine. Eric had once joked that the milkman and postman must have overstayed their welcome one morning, and Ellie remembered flushing furiously when he'd said it.

She'd never been able to bury the memory of the kitchen fitter, who had sired her middle daughter in an affair which had lasted all of four minutes, quite deep enough. Even if she'd wanted to try, she would never be able to recall his name. She'd never known it. All she could remember was the broadness of his tanned chest and the coarseness of both his stubbled chin and his language.

"It was the pressure, you see. The strain of looking after your big sister. Your daddy and I were arguing a lot because of it. I needed something. Somebody. ANYbody. But it's so unlike me. It really is. I still don't know why it happened", she had once told the four-year-old Karen whom she knew was too young to understand. No-one would understand. That was the problem.

It was the only time Ellie had ever unburdened herself of her shame and was a necessary exorcism as she slumped in the troughs of post-natal depression after the birth of Nina.

She'd regretted her confession many times since. Ellie couldn't help but wonder if the memory of her confession lay cloaked in Karen's subconscious. Had this precipitated her rebelliousness, she feared? Never once did Ellie consider that she may have driven her to it by her prejudices.

Karen's voice brought Ellie back to the present.

"We-ell", Karen drawled, choosing her words as carefully as she'd considered Anna's letter. "If you don't buy a ticket, you won't win the raffle".

Anna looked at her blankly, miscomprehension written all over her face. "Yes – but do you like?"

"I like it, yes. But it's not going to win. At least you'll get a signed photo as consolation, though".

"But I don't want a signed photo. I want Dexter".

Karen leaned across and ruffled her sister's greasy hair with one hand whilst flicking back her own fringe with the other. With a gentle smile on her face, Karen concluded "Sorry, Anna, but you ain't going to get him".

Ellie grudgingly admired Karen's honesty yet couldn't help reigning against her. "You never know – she might".

"Mum. Don't build her hopes up. You know she'll only be more disappointed. Why not be honest? You know as well as I do that, although it's a good try", she winked at Anna, "it's not going to win".

Ellie bit her tongue. Contented herself with asking Karen if she'd at least type the letter up for her sister and e-mail the entry to the magazine's publishing house. Told her it was the bare minimum she could do after disappointing her.

It was Nina that spoke. "No point in that, Mum. They're not accepting e-mail entries".

"Why ever not? Don't tell me that they are actually going to use Royal Mail? Good for them. Encouraging young people to write proper letters. There's hope for us all yet."

Nina laughed. "Not quite, mum. Someone's hacked into their system. They've shut it down until it gets the all-clear from the police. Worried the mailing list of all these teenagers gets out. Paedos would have a field day so they've temporarily gone back to postal entries".

Ellie shuddered. "Good God. What's the world come to?"

"Anyway, Anna", Karen said rising to leave. "D'ya want me to post it for you?"

Anna's face brightened. She stepped to the old-fashioned bureau, selected a first-class stamp specifically for the bright blue kingfisher depicted above the R.S.P.B motif, and waddled back to Karen.

Anna saw Karen to the door whilst Ellie breathed a sigh of relief. A visit from Karen without a major bust-up was a rare thing these days.

What's more, she hadn't even voiced a complaint or asked for a favour. In fact, Ellie didn't know why Karen had called in at all. A look of puzzlement spread over Ellie's face but was stifled by the return of Anna.

Smiling broadly, Anna jabbed a podgy finger at Karen's photograph. "I AM going to win", she said, "Regardless of what SHE thinks".

Meanwhile, at the end of the road, Karen sifted through her shoulder bag. She produced two envelopes, studied them for a moment, then posted one.

She slipped the other, with a distinctive kingfisher stamp, back into her bag.

CHAPTER THREE

Every morning for the next three weeks it was Anna, not Nina, who was first to reach the mail as it dropped onto the hallway laminate. With each day, her enthusiasm waned only slightly but the cumulative effect was noticeable.

Anna became irritable, even snapped at her mother once or twice, and Nina made a point of being absent around mail time. Ellie wished the competition had never existed as her once cheerful daughter changed day-by-day.

Then, on the twenty-second morning, together with the electricity account and a catalogue circular came an envelope addressed in bold type to 'MISS ANNA DARNELL'.

Anna squealed with delight. She clattered into the lounge holding the envelope aloft as if she were a standard-bearer in a Roman legion.

"It's here, Mum. Look, it's here. It's got my name on it. This is it. Mum, I'm so excited. My hands are shaky. Look. I'm all wobbly. I really am". The words spilled from her like champagne from a shaken bottle.

Ellie watched with trepidation, waiting and wondering how Anna would react to the realisation that she was once more a loser in life when she produced an autographed portrait from the envelope.

And Anna did react. But not in the way Ellie anticipated. She looked on as her daughter's eyes widened, almost protruded from their sockets. Anna's mouth lolled open not in its usual vacuous way but in an uncontrollable expression of glee. She flung her arms as if in an early attempt at aviation, compounded the imagery by leaping high in the air. She landed with such force that Ellie's Victorian ladies tumbled from their mantelpiece haven.

Ellie Darnell watched with growing astonishment as Anna shrieked "I've done it. I'VE DONE IT! I'm meeting Dexter – I told you I'd win, didn't I, Mum? Eh? Didn't I? Nina…Nina! I've WON; I've REALLY won!!"

The decibel level hardly subsided as she raced upstairs to rouse her slumbering sister, the victim of one-too-many dry whites.

Ellie sat back in her chair, stunned. 'It's a hoax. It's got to be', she said aloud to herself. 'If that's what those two were up to, Heaven help them'.

Now certain of her suspicions as the initial disbelief waned, Ellie reached down for the discarded envelope as Anna thundered around upstairs, the din sufficient to raise the dead if not quite her hungover sister.

Ellie checked the postmark. 'LONDON'. She read the headed notepaper. 'DEXTYLE'. Shook her head to clear it, and checked again. Yes, postmarked London still.

Finally, whilst bedlam continued above, reality descended below as Ellie accepted the evidence in front of her. Somehow, her daughter had indeed won and her letter would be printed for the adolescent world to read in the next edition of 'Dextyle'.

'It sure is a funny old world', Ellie mused as she set about restoring order to the chaos created in her living room.

**

Ellie Darnell struggled through the front door, both arms extended by the heavy shopping bags in each hand.

"I'm back, Anna – help me with this shopping, will y— Oh, it's you", she said, her brow furrowed by the sight of Karen stood next to Nina in the passage way.

"Just passing by, Mum", she said by way of explanation, tossing back her fringe.

"You've never 'just passed by' here in your life. Why start now?"

The brief exchange was interrupted by the plop of the evening newspaper as it hit the deck in its fall from the letterbox. This was followed by a second, heavier object which balanced in the metallic jaw for a moment before plummeting downwards.

Nina took a half-stride forward only to be stopped in her tracks when Karen's arm gently extended across her. Anna bounded past them like an excitable puppy and, as Ellie looked towards her, she missed the reassuring half-smile Karen gave her younger sister.

Ellie watched with swelling pride as Anna flicked through her fanzine until her eyes found what they sought. A smile remained on Ellie's face even after Anna's face had changed; changed to the expression she had expected to see the previous week.

Anna's chubby cheeks reddened. Her eyes watered. A heart-rending sob emerged from her throat. With disbelief and miscomprehension, Ellie watched and heard her eldest race upstairs to the sanctuary of her room.

Ellie Darnell bent and picked up the fanzine. She read not the disjointed letter her daughter had submitted but a lucid, well-crafted piece of rare humour which, while poking gentle tongue-in-cheek fun at the whole 'Dextyle' craze, was nevertheless a glowing eulogy of Monroe himself.

It was as if a curtain had opened in front of Ellie's eyes. She lowered the magazine and looked at her offspring. Nina cast the nervous glance of a timid mouse at Karen, who looked directly back into her mother's eyes.

"You bitches. You total, absolute BITCHES", Ellie hissed. "How could you do this to your own sister?"

Nina sobbed noiselessly. "We only entered for Anna's sake. We never thought we'd win, but…"

"But you did", Ellie finished the sentence for her. "You – not Anna, but YOU. Can't you see that?"

"Bullshit". Karen spoke for the first time.

Tears of fury welled in her mother's eyes. "What did you just say?"

"You heard. I said 'bullshit'. Anna wanted to win this competition more than anything in the world. All she wanted to do was meet Dexter; just to meet him. Just once. And WE gave her that chance".

"All she wanted to do? Don't tell me that that was 'all she wanted to do'. I'll show you how much she wanted to meet Dexter Monroe. Come here!". Ellie reached out with both hands, one on Nina's sleeve, the other grasped the collar of Karen's sweatshirt.

Family portraits were knocked askew in the stairwell as her daughters struggled against her grip. Nina flinched and cowered like a beaten dog as her mother dragged them upstairs, spinning them around the spiral staircase so quickly Nina's head swam. Ellie pulled the girls across the landing until the trio confronted Anna's closed bedroom door.

Ellie Darnell and Nina were red-eyed as the matriarch flung open the door. The finger she pointed at the bed trembled like a flame in the wind.

"That's how much she wanted to meet Dexter-bloody-Monroe. Look!"

Three pairs of eyes rested upon the prostate figure, legs kicking the air, fists pounding her own body like a Mullah in purdah.

Nina averted her streaming eyes. She couldn't bear to see her sister like this. Even Karen, street hardened as she was, swallowed hard though she alone remained dry-eyed.

"Stop it, Mum. Stop it", Nina pleaded. "I only did it because I love her so much".

"You've got a goddamn funny way of showing it, my girl", Ellie said, a touch more evenly.

But her fury returned when Karen spoke. "That's not fair, Mum".

"Not fair? You think this is FAIR?", Ellie demanded of her, pointing again at Anna. The smell of stale urine hung in the air like a wet towel. "You've taken all she had left. You've taken the poor girl's pride".

Nina's eyes stung as if she'd swam in a chlorine-rich pool. "I do love her, Mum", she said. "But I've never been able to do anything for her. She's my sister but I can't play with her or even have a proper conversation with her. I'm embarrassed and I hate myself for it. I've got everything: a future, marriage, children. I've got it all to look forward to. But what has Anna got? She's got nothing".

Ellie's temper was becalmed by an overwhelming pride in her youngest. She wanted to take her in her arms, smother her with love and affection. But then Karen had to go and spoil everything.

"Look, we shouldn't be saying this in front of Anna. It'll only make her feel worse".

That was all it needed to rekindle Ellie's fury. Although she directed her abuse at Karen, the anger she felt was aimed at herself. 'Goddamnit', she thought. 'I should've said that, not that bitching daughter of mine'.

Ellie bundled the two girls downstairs where Karen continued to win the battle with her emotions. "Nina's not the only one, you know", her rebel daughter said. "I love you both, too".

"Ha. You've just GOT to be joking. Breaking everything up by leaving us for that hobo of yours".

"Leave Danny out of this. That's not the reason I left. You know it wasn't. You made me leave. You've never had time for me. Never. I've had to feed off scraps of affection my entire life. Well, I found someone who showed me what I'd been missing all these years. Danny, that's who I found".

Ellie returned the serve with equal ferocity. "Oh, so Danny gives you everything I couldn't, does he? Danny who's never had a job in his life. Danny who you've supported. Danny who's never even set foot in this house. Danny who saw you coming a mile off and hung onto you like a limpet".

"Yes, Mum; that's right. All of it is. But you forgot to add 'Danny who cares for me. Danny who's shown me the love and tenderness you never have".

As they continued to trade insults with each other, a neighbour banged on the wall. Ellie reached down for the nearest object and flung it towards the wall, shouting after it "Keep out of this. It's none of your business" as the Faience figurine shattered in a snowstorm of fine pieces.

"Yes, Mum", Karen continued, still holding herself together. "All of what you say is true. But so is everything I said. Including the bit about loving you. Despite everything. I feel guilty as Hell walking out. But I had to. For all our sakes. And I did what I did because I wanted Anna to be happy. If Anna was happy, you'd be happy. And you deserve it. I mean that. I really do".

The argument rolled on. The figure of Anna peeked through the staircase spindles, unseen by the protagonists. She crept silently to the hall. Stood in the doorway watching the argument rage.

"How can I be happy?", Ellie answered Karen's statement. She was blinded by tears. Wiped them away, then accepted she'd lost the battle as they were replaced by still more. "I've no-one. No-one".

"Don't be like that, Mum", Karen comforted. "Daddy would want you to be happy; want you to have fun..."

A vision of a kitchen fitter sprang into Ellie's minds-eye, and leapt out again just as quickly to avoid the vicious slap aimed at him by Ellie.

But Karen wasn't so quick. The blow struck her high on the cheekbone, spinning her round. Her fringe flopped wildly in front of her eyes and, for once, it wasn't flicked back.

Ellie gasped in horror. Brought her hand to her mouth in an involuntary gesture. Watched the red imprint of a hand blossom on Karen's face. An imprint of her hand. On her daughter's face.

Tears came like a breached dam. But they were the tears of the assailant, not the victim.

"Oh my God, my God", Ellie whispered, hand still pressed to her mouth. "My baby, my baby. I'm sorry. Oh, my baby…" she raced forward, taking Karen in a tight bear-hug. Nina, eyes shot red, joined the embrace.

Anna moved with a fluidity she'd never felt before. She stepped to the wine table that was home to the telephone. She brought an object up close to her myopic eyes. It was a crumpled letter with a London postmark. Anna picked up the telephone and dialled the number on the letterhead.

The bruise on Karen's cheek bloomed. Ellie put her hand to it. She didn't know what else to say other than "I really am so sorry". The words came in a whisper.

Karen said nothing. Just nodded. Pursed her lips in the semblance of a smile but gently removed her mother's hand from her face.

From the doorway came Anna's almost inaudible voice. "It's ok now, mum".

"What, darling?", whispered Ellie, her voice breaking.

"It's ok", reassured Anna. "I've just rung the phone number on the letter and told them I don't want their stinking, rotten prize".

Her mother and sisters looked at her in silence.

"Why ever not?", Ellie finally managed to stutter.

"Well, Mum, it would be cheating, wouldn't it? And you wouldn't want me to cheat, Mummy".

Ellie screwed her eyes tight. That goddamn labourer again. "No, darling. I wouldn't want you to cheat", she said. Her voice broke with emotion and unbridled pride. She held out an arm and welcomed Anna into her embrace. Through watery eyes, she saw that Nina had begun to weep again so she signalled for her to join them.

"Mum?", Anna's voice enquired hesitatingly.

"Yes, darling?"

"Can I have a party instead?"

"Yes, darling. You can have a party".

Ellie caught sight of Karen and watched her wipe at a single tear drop as it meandered its lonely way down her cheek.

CHAPTER FOUR

Bank Holiday weekend. Ellie lay back in her favourite chair. Her eyes were closed and a relaxed, almost serene, smile played on her face.

Peals of girlish laughter rang around her home. Music throbbed from three different sources, all different tunes; an electronic medley of contrasts that, several weeks ago, would have jarred Ellie's frayed nerves as surely as a dentist's drill. Now, though, she found it faintly amusing.

She opened her eyes. Noticed the stem of a wine glass tilted at a precarious angle between her fingertips and cared not one iota that her wine may spill and stain the carpet.

Anna, she noticed, flitted between guests. She held a tray of party food and offered it around. The perfect hostess. For the first time in her life, Anna sparkled. Nina had applied some make up to Anna and curled her hair for her. Normally shy and reticent, Anna was loving her moment in the spotlight.

She mixed freely with her cousins. Made sure her friends from the day centre she attended were comfortable and at ease. Fussed over a baby boy sat in the corner with his mother. Dropped sandwich fillings and cream cake on the lap of said mother without breaking into tears. Generally, behaved 'all grown up'.

Ellie's smile matched the happy grin on her eldest's face. She went to drink a toast to her then realised she'd emptied her glass. Ellie sought out another bottle in the kitchen.

There, she found Nina sitting on a worktop. She had a face buried in her neck, the owner's hands running through her hair. Nina rolled her eyes as if to say he's got no chance.

Ellie laughed and raised her empty glass to her daughter. Yes, she'd been aptly named; both 'pretty' and 'beautiful eyed'. Ellie sniggered to herself at the irony. 'Nina' may suit her but it was pure good fortune.

Eric had chosen the names for both Anna and Karen; Anna named after his mother, Karen because Ellie had been convinced she was having a boy and had the name Darren already chosen. Eric called her Karen simply because it rhymed.

So it fell to Ellie to choose a name for the third child. Mrs Darnell had studied Tolstoy at school and, with an Anna and a Karen on board, it just had to be 'Nina', didn't it?

Fortunately, Eric hadn't realised the connection until too late or he would have insisted on something else. And then pretty, beautiful-eyed Nina wouldn't have had the name she deserved.

Back in the sanctuary of her armchair, for the first time Ellie was struck by another significance in the girls' names. Tolstoy's novel portrayed family life as a source of comfort and happiness. Something Ellie had never enjoyed. Until now. The thought sobered her.

She wished Karen could have been there with them. Not that the rift remained. Far from it. It was early days in their reconciliation but reconciled they were. But Karen had pre-arranged plans. She was away for the weekend. Manchester, Ellie seemed to recall. Some festival or other. It was a sign of their improved relationship that Ellie didn't mind. She fully understood and genuinely believed Karen when she had expressed her regret.

But Ellie wasn't going to allow herself to become melancholy. This was a new beginning for them all. Somewhere in the mix of music, Ellie recognised a tune. A familiar voice sang a familiar line.

"Loneliness is a crowded room".

Ellie looked around her packed living room. "Not any more it, it isn't. Not any more", she said.

Feeling a little foolish when guests looked in her direction, she was relieved when they turned away at the sound of the doorbell. No-one went to answer.

"I'll get that, then, will I?", she smiled. Her head swam when she got to her feet and she gripped the arms of her chair to steady herself. Too much wine.

She took her time getting to the door. So much so that the bell rang again just as she reached it.

"All right. I'm here now. Patience would be good". The door swung open. "Karen!", Ellie trilled. "Oh Karen. I thought you couldn't make it. I'm so happy you managed to get back in time. Anna will be over the moon".

She looked at the tall girl alongside Karen.

"And you've brought a friend, too. Good. Hello. Pleased to meet you. I'm Ellie. Karen's Mum". She extended a hand towards the smiling girl, who glanced towards Karen.

"Mum", said Karen. She hesitated for a heartbeat. "Mum, this is Danielle. Danni." A pause to let it sink in. "It's time you knew. I've wanted to tell you but you; well, you just assumed."

Ellie's hand retracted like a snapped elastic band.

The smile flickered for a moment. Then, instead of offering Danni her hand, she put her arms around her and pulled her towards her. She kissed Danni on both cheeks.

"Come in. Come in. Don't just stand there. I've heard so much about you. Welcome to the family, Danni. Let's introduce you to everyone."

Karen stayed in the doorway for a moment as her mother led Danni inside. Then, she crumpled to the floor, releasing a lifetime of emotions.

****

ABOUT THE AUTHOR

Colin Youngman is a true Geordie (born within sound of the tugboats on the River Tyne), and now lives in Northumberland.

His first work was published at the age of 9 when a contribution to children's comic Sparky brought him the rich rewards of a 10/- Postal Order and a transistor radio. Since then, his material has featured in outlets as diverse as national newspapers, sports magazines, and travel guides, all whilst developing a career as a Senior Executive in the Public Sector.

Colin specializes in mystery / thriller novels whilst his shorter fiction crosses genres, from thriller to mystery, fantasy to horror, family drama to humour.

His novellas fall in a niche ideal for the commuter or traveller.

Colin also works as a TV Supporting Artiste and has been approached for roles in ITV crime serial Vera and period drama Victoria.

Follow him on Twitter @seewhy59

Printed in Great Britain
by Amazon